Ancient Oceans of Central Kentucky

a novel by

DAVID CONNERLEY NAHM

TWO DOLLAR RADIO
Books too loud to ignore.

TWO DOLLAR RADIO is a family-run outfit founded in 2005 with the mission to reaffirm the cultural and artistic spirit of the publishing industry.

We aim to do this by presenting bold works of literary merit, each book, individually and collectively, providing a sonic progression that we believe to be too loud to ignore.

Cover: *Collecting Rocks And Shells Along The Banks Of The Ohio River, June 1972,* by William Strode. U.S. National Archives.
Fossils: *Kentucky Fossil Shells, A Monograph of the Fossil Shells of the Silurian and Devonian Rocks of Kentucky,* by Henry Nettelroth, C. E., 1889.
Author photograph: Jennifer Connerley

Typeset in Garamond, the best font ever.
Printed in the United States of America.

TWO DOLLAR RADIO
Books too loud to ignore.
www.TwoDollarRadio.com
twodollar@TwoDollarRadio.com

For JLC

But who knows the fate of his bones,
or how often he is to be buried?

—Sir Thomas Browne, *Urn Burial*

Ancient Oceans

of Central

Kentucky

PROLOGUE: THE CHILDREN'S CHOIR

In Sunday's lengthening shadows, neighborhood children lounge by the hip-high brick wall that surrounds the town cemetery and they tell strange stories to stall the night's trundle. "Listen," they say. "Wait, listen." Their neighborhood is boring and their houses are boring and their parents are boring. One points, saying, "That grave is empty," and it is. They've heard all of these stories before—at the end of a dark hall during a church lock-in, from cousins on a dock at the lake, in hushes between songs during choir practice, on walks home from school, during the roar of lunch, in the backseats of buses, over telephones with coiling cords tangling around wrists. And now, with the last exhalation of summer they tell them again.

"My brother says—"

At the far end of the cemetery, there is a man lingering along the edge of the shadow cast by the maples. The children cackle and socks slip down ankles. They caw, guffawing, leaping and leaning, kicking stones to quell rushing blood and billows of nervous laughter. The man has stopped by a marble mausoleum and he just stands and watches the children. In the distance unseen cars pass and pop songs boom. They sneak glances to try and tell who it is standing behind the stones, but they never get a good look at him and later when they talk about it, they all remember something different. And then summer is gone before they know it and it is fall. "Look," they say. "Listen."

Stories without end or ending. This was the first summer they spent listening to songs to which they are not allowed to listen. They holler out car windows at a pitiful-looking woman walking by the cemetery gate, filthy hair and grim face comically made-up. Their lungs rip with laughter and red cheeks wet. And then the fall is gone and the winter comes slinking in on the low sky. They dream of older brothers and sisters in growling cars, harrowing empty nights with windows down and radio squall like a pillar of fire into the night. They had cousins from the city spend a weekend teaching them how to dance, telling them about the girls and boys they knew who slipped out and stole through the night to throw rocks at the window of some possible love still slumbering. Maybe it will snow. Maybe it won't. Maybe the man can hear their voices and maybe he watches them slink in the sinking sunlight. The rain washes the names off of the old limestone markers and only the water rises heavenward again. During a caesura in their talk, they look up and the man is gone.

"That grave is empty." They gasp and giggle and then, just like that, it is dark and they can no longer see each other and no longer hear the distant love songs of passing cars and a voice calls a name and they rise up, running toward home.

LEAH SHEPHERD DIDN'T KNOW THE NAME OF the song the bald man in horn-rimmed glasses was singing to himself as he stared at her through the snow. She thought of the muffled songs of the cars that would pass outside of the windows of the bedroom she shared with her brother Jacob when they were children. The cars cresting the hill, headlights filling the bedroom for a moment with racing trapezoids of white and those brief harmonies as the cars doppler past and then silence again and dark. Sometimes she would hear a sliver of melody that she would recognize, but she was too young to know its name and it slipped from her mind as soon as the world outside their bedroom was still again.

The man stared down at her from a distance, backlit by his own headlights, and she had that feeling again, the melody's name just out of reach, and the air glittered around them.

Wind frisked through the trees, bending new branches and sending the light green leaves like ticker-tape to the ground of the woods behind the apartment building on the edge of Crow Station, Kentucky, where Leah Shepherd, the executive director of a nonprofit organization which provided emergency support services to low income women and children, lived. Her apartment: nine-hundred square feet, one bed, one bath, kitchen, open concept, $600/mo., good light, NO PETS.

She woke and stretched and dressed and drove to the old house that had been subdivided into offices in the small, damp downtown. The old house needed to be painted and needed the half-rotted wood handrails to be repaired, but the budget did not allow for these needs to be addressed this year and likely would not allow for them to be addressed next year either. Charitable giving was down. Federal and state funds were cut. Grants were scarce. The baseboards were separating from the floor and the carpet runners were threadbare. The chairs at the conference table were worn when donated years before by a law firm in town and were now, after several repairs, bordering on hazardous. There was a kitchen filled with mismatched plastic plates and stained coffee pots and non-dairy creamers of unknown vintage. Leah sat and listened and signed papers and took calls and drove back to the apartment as the blue sky faded and lowered.

Behind her apartment building there ran a stream and in the evenings Leah would walk in the woods that rose along the stream's banks. She walked to try and lose the day, to lose the women and children she'd seen sitting in the waiting room, to lose the tales of unpaid water bills and cut-off electricity and of bruises and wailing children and the giggling half-truths and sob stories and excuses and the hungry look on the quiet children that played with toys only donated to the nonprofit after they couldn't be sold at a yard sale—quarters, dimes, nickels, nothing. She walked to lose all of this and water rushed over rocks, colorful garbage caught in fallen branches fluttered, bits of blue between bare branches, capering plastic tatters. Later, she slipped off her shoes by the door and slipped her dirty dishes into the empty sink while listening to the radio for company and though she thought that she'd walked them all out of her mind, she remembered the letters she'd signed and the arms she'd touched and the grants that she needed to finish applying for and she rubbed her face and walked into her bedroom and undressed and got into bed and closed her eyes and it was all still with her.

In the mirror of the bathroom beneath the stairs at work, Leah straightened her blouse and catalogued the creases in her face that she'd never really noticed before. On the telephone once, she'd been asked to describe herself and had struggled to do so. The women came and waited to meet with her, their children swinging legs, bubbling with questions, begging to be taken to the toy store, to the ice cream shop, to the fair that will open that night. Broken spines of discarded books left open on empty seats. Leah smiled and listened and signed forms. She heard a woman tell her son that if he was good he could go and Leah turned and asked, "You're going to the fair? That sounds like so much fun. I haven't been to a fair in forever. Are you excited?" As she was saying this, she felt a tremor through her body. She'd not thought of the fair in decades and it rose electric before her, obscuring for a moment the child's face. The lights in Shaker frenzy and the thunderous din of voices and the smell of greasy food that seemed to have completely displaced the air itself. The child writhed and looked up at his mother for what he should say. Any good child has a natural fear of strange adults.

In meetings with her staff, she discussed possible sources of support, reviewed the increase in requests for help. Outside of the window of her office a tall woman with filthy hair walked by, but Leah, in a reverie, didn't notice her. The caw of the telephone on her desk, the red light of line three trilling, brought her back from wherever she'd been and her hand went to the nape of her neck when the wind rattled the drafty windows of the old office or when it called to her through the trees. There was a birthmark in the shape of a crab underneath her hair, hidden by crimped tresses. In the meetings she nodded and sighed over the names and numbers. In the kitchen, late in the afternoon, the receptionist, a widow who boarded college students in a basement apartment, rank with mildew, said, as she poured a cup of decaf and cut a comically small piece of pound cake that someone had brought the day before, "I didn't know you have a brother." Leah looked up from the window, startled, and said, "He passed away." The receptionist apologized and said she'd put a call through for Leah's voicemail, but must have misunderstood what the man said. When Leah returned to her office there wasn't any message.

When she was thirteen, her parents took her to the beach. Just the three of them. She didn't like to go in the water. Rather, she preferred to sit in the sand and build elaborate drizzle-decorated castles around her legs, though her mother told her she was too old. "Honey, you're too old for that," her mother would say. "Don't you want to get in the water? Or go to the arcade on the pier? I've got quarters." Every time the water would creep closer and closer and eventually suck the sand away from between her legs. Even when she built a dam with her interlaced fingers to catch what she'd built, it would slither through, taking the dam with it. Coquina clams nibbled at her skin. One evening her father walked her to the arcade at the pier, her shorts heavy with quarters dredged from her mother's purse. They didn't talk as they walked along and when they got there, he left her by the bright door of the gameroom and walked down to the end of the pier by himself and looked out at the rising night. Leah stood with the crazed moths in the glow of the lights by the door and watched the teenagers furiously pounding buttons and wrenching joysticks back and forth, desperate to elude the paths of increasingly erratic ghosts. Some boys wearing nothing but swim trunks, their hair matted with dried salt around their ears and broken-out foreheads said something that she did not hear and began to laugh at her. Their voices battered at the lights. From where she stood, she could not see her father at the end of the pier and she must have begun to cry because the boys were howling at her tears. She did not like to go into the water and she did not like to go to the pier. Leah preferred to stay in the sand.

There was more than one stream in more than one wood, more than one wall of sand around more than one pair of legs, more than one woman watching rainwater erode the banks where she walked. Leah worried about this until late at night, eventually falling asleep on the couch. The radio station fell to static.

At the Harrod County Fair, Leah Shepherd and her little brother Jacob waited their turn to ride the rusted Zipper. Their father was somewhere in the shadows on the other side of the contraption, waiting for his children. Cars flipped and spun in the dark, the machine flashing red and white, children moaning, pleading to be let off, causing a filigree of laughter from below.

By the gate to get onto the ride, boys in pegged jeans and sleeveless t-shirts spat onto the straw-covered ground. "Wanna come with us?" one asked as the others stalked and hunched in the glitter of the ride's light, but Leah declined, unnerved by the boys' open stares, by the boys' glistening foreheads and erupting cheeks. She searched the dark for some sign of their father, but he'd wandered off. Jacob was dazzled by the figures capering in the din and squeezed his big sister's hand.

The boys howled. In their pockets, eye droppers of gin. They skipped to their car with eyes wide open and sped into the night, down gray country roads, grieving over nothing they could name, beating the dashboard with their fists. Near dawn they broke into a cemetery and pissed on the first angel they could find.

Leah Shepherd waited in her car for the light to change to some other color so she could continue her short drive to work. Her morning's mouth yawned and she checked her cell phone, but there weren't any messages. A gaggle of girls crossed in the crosswalk and the radio announcer said, *Go ahead, caller. Hello? Go ahead. Are you there? Caller?* Dew limned lawns with the new sun. The light changed, but still she waited for a filthy-looking woman carrying a battered backpack to cross in front of her. She waited, then she went, and the radio cut to commercial.

In the thin trees by the stream, an empty lighter, ruined clothes, and a tarp up on branches to keep it all dry.

Leah spent the morning reading the Internet and avoiding people telling her how nice the picture of her in the newspaper looked. She smiled and said, "Thank you," but inside wished that no one would say anything. Not that the award meant much. It was a cheap plaque engraved at the local sporting goods store, the kind of thing that local Chambers of Commerce give out by the bushel, and it had only been published because the Crow Station newspaper had temporarily run out of stories about stray dogs in the library or new appliance stores opening on the bypass.

A few days later, as she was on her way out the backdoor to lunch, the receptionist buzzed her office and said that a man was here to see her. He didn't have an appointment and wouldn't say what his business was. Leah didn't recognize his name, but assumed he was the husband or boyfriend or father of one of the poor women she was working with, and having no desire to deal with whoever it was, having already spent the morning with a woman with two little children who would not stop fighting with one another, no matter how many times the woman promised that she would switch them, Leah told the receptionist to tell the man that she wasn't available and slipped out to lunch. Despite this, the man found her where she was eating. "Leah?"

Even in the most long and lovely days of summer, Leah and Jacob Shepherd were content to laze indoors, reading or watching television or wrestling perilously close to the top of the stairs. At her wits end, Mrs. Shepherd would shoo them outside where their indoor irises would scream in outdoor light. "It is too pretty to stay inside," she would say, remembering how she'd spent summer nights sleeping in tall grass with her sisters.

The yards of the houses on their street were cluttered with trees, the trunks of which were dressed in soft gowns of moss. The trees crowded so thick that most of the houses were completely hidden from the street, only their crumbling walks disappearing on their way to dim doors still visible to Leah and Jacob. They sat outside in their backyard, the sun napping on their skin and Jacob would ask Leah to tell him a story and Leah would warn him that she only knew scary stories and he would promise not to get scared this time and she would tell him, knowing full well that he would quickly become too terrified to listen to more. She grinned as the horror slowly began to creep across his face and at her own ability to conjure gore that was still, at ten years old, only speculative to her.

The voice of the breeze and a click-clack of boxcars at the edge of town. The all-invading wafts of stock-yard stalls. Wind rattles oak and sumac. A mackerel sky, and thus, three days dry. When the sun sets, there will be ribbons of pink.

One summer morning, Mr. Shepherd took Leah and Jacob for a walk to the school where he worked so that he could show them the human skeleton that was kept in a utility closet in the basement. Mr. Shepherd held Leah up so that she could touch its jaw, but Jacob, unable to even enter the room, sat in the stairwell alone with a pus on, half-heartedly moaning and begging to be taken home. "Don't be a baby," Mr. Shepherd called down the hall to his seven-year-old son. "This is really neat." Jacob's choice was utterly absurd to Leah—the dark stairwell was far more frightening than the skeleton in the closet. She chattered her teeth and listened to the sound clatter in her ears. Leah watched Jacob while Mr. Shepherd walked upstairs. They waited for a while, looking at the things on shelves, Jacob trying not to look at the skeleton in the corner, Leah taking his hand and telling him funny stories about the preserved biological specimens they found themselves among. A box of brachiopods and trilobites. They waited for their father for what felt like a very long time and then went looking for him, adventuring through the dark halls of the summer-emptied high school, imagining themselves characters in a forgotten folktale, left by their father in a cave of corpses, set free and seeking safety in a grim and dark castle. Distant howls and cries. They crept up the stairs toward a dim hallway and heard a voice, distant and low, and they knew that they'd found the horrific heart of the crumbling maze and would have to face the creature that writhed there. They peeked around the corner, to see what they could see. Their father was standing in the door of a classroom in a shaft of light, talking to someone unseen. When he saw his children down at the end of the hall, he got angry and asked them how long they'd been there.

On the way home, Jacob ran ahead of his father and sister, despite Mr. Shepherd's barking. The boy ran down an embankment to the stream that followed the sidewalk through town. He was moving far too fast and tumbled into the shallow water, startling a paddling of ducks. The stream bent and bowed through town. Jacob yelped and flailed and Leah looked up at her father, but Mr. Shepherd just shrugged and said, "The Creature from the Black Lagoon has him now. There's nothing we can do." And he took his daughter's hand and walked on home. Leah worried about Jacob the whole way, right up until he appeared on the doorstep, just after them, drenched and scowling.

That night, the pizza had mushrooms on it and Jacob began to cry because he was scared of mushrooms. He was scared of mushrooms because his father told him that mushrooms were man's only natural predator. It had been a day of indignities.

At night, in the room they shared, Leah could make out a sliver of song, a muffled voice in mid-phrase, a lonesome love song fading as a car passed. Their room faced the street and the light from passing cars spilled in the corners. "Are you scared of anything?" Jacob asked and Leah said, "No." Jacob leaned over and looked out of the window next to his bed and then said, "Not even the man in our yard?"

"There isn't anyone in our yard."

"Uh huh. I can see him. He's in the shadows." Later, Leah could hear Jacob snoring as she listened for the sound of the backdoor opening slowly, the pained creak like an old jaw.

The next day, while Mrs. Shepherd was ironing in the bedroom and Jacob was watching *Emergency*, Leah poured a small paper cup of water on his mattress and then promptly tattled on Jacob for wetting the bed. Unfortunately, Leah had failed to pour some on the crotch of his pajamas as well and she'd received the paddling instead from her mother while Jacob sashayed around the house. That night, while he was in the bath, she scratched the record about Zacchaeus that he liked to listen to while riding his rocking horse. A few hours later, when he put the record on the Fisher-Price player, it skipped, a voice singing *wee wee wee wee wee* endlessly and in the moment just before Jacob began to cry, as he registered that his favorite record was ruined, Leah felt a terrible twist of shame for what she'd done and she put her arms around her little brother and comforted him. Without a confession, she offered to give him her two favorite records— *Monster Mash* and *The Mouse Factory*—and he was overjoyed. *I am a happy mouse and I ought to be.* They were without a doubt the two best records in the house and now they were his. That night Jacob slept with them in his bed. *We are happy kids.*

One night, a summer night, thirty-some years later, Leah slept with the window open in her apartment, a window facing the parking lot and Leah woke to a woman's scream. She rose in the light of streetlamps and looked out at the empty lot, at the distant trees, listened to the breeze, listened again for the voice, but if it had ever been there, it was gone, lost to the trees. Leah wondered if she should go out and see if someone was in danger, if there was something wrong, but not hearing anything else, she realized that it was just as likely a scream of joy and she went back to bed, but not before sitting at the open window in the dark for several minutes, listening.

Isolated, house-bound, no visitors, children barely sparing the time to call days after her birthday or before Christmas, the old woman slipped and fell down basement stairs. She kept a small workshop down in the basement where she made figurines for the children at church. Despite Leah's pleading, the woman continued to slowly slump herself up and down the steep wooden steps into the pale fluorescent light in worn slippers on a daily basis. Until the day her ankles gave out on the third from top step. And then a week went by. All agreed it was terrible.

The way the woman passed made the house difficult to sell, much to the chagrin of the beneficiaries of the estate who would call and ask the executor when they would receive their share. "It isn't that I care about the money. I just want some closure." There had been several offers on the house, but they'd been rejected. "It isn't the money. It was the house we grew up in and I know how much my father put into it and what it meant to him and what it means to us and what it should be worth and

I don't want to sell it until we find a buyer who appreciates what it means to us." It wasn't about the money.

The woman went to Leah's church, and Leah, feeling sorry for the woman's lonely life, her curved back and knuckles in gnarls like pallid roots, would visit on weekends, picking up groceries on the way, or on Sundays when it was her turn to take shut-in communion. There were several little old ladies that Leah had done this for over the years, old church ladies whose husbands had gone on, or women who'd never married, living on fixed incomes in small houses, women who would smile at her before their minds could remember who she was, if they ever did. They were just happy to see someone. Leah was happy to sit and not talk.

Leah put the groceries away and warned the woman about the basement steps. She called the woman after a severe storm and cleared the yard of broken branches. Leah listened to the woman talk about her children, off in other states with good jobs and lousy spouses and spoiled children. Beautiful, but spoiled. Leah smiled at her, held her hand, listened to the long day drain in the clock in the foyer and petted the woman's poodle. The dog was missing an eye. It would fix that socket on Leah and no matter how much Leah wanted to turn away, she could not. The poor thing just wanted her to pay attention to it. Leah felt sad for the woman when the poor thing finally passed, though Leah was secretly relieved to be free of its gazing socket.

She spent many days like this, listening to the woman and petting the dog and watching the long light.

Then one afternoon, Leah knocked on the door, but there was no answer. She opened the door with the key she kept and called the woman's name, but there was no answer. She set the bag of groceries on the counter and called down the basement steps, where a light was on, but there was no answer. Leah wondered if the woman had called out to her and had died upset that Leah had not come.

Before her death, the old woman had executed a new will that left Leah a substantial cash bequest. The woman's children, whom Leah had never spoken with, despite having tried to contact the woman's oldest son once, alleged that Leah obtained the change in their mother's will through undue influence. Furthermore, the Estate alleged that Leah had withdrawn money from the old woman's bank account and spent the money on herself. Leah admitted that she had withdrawn the money, but had done so for the old woman, but Leah had given her cash and no receipts to prove it. In the end, Leah spent a substantial amount on an attorney who recommended, in light of the circumstances, settling the matter. The suit was something that caused the board of directors of the nonprofit some concern. It wasn't that they believed that she'd done anything untoward, quite the contrary, all believed her to be of the highest professional and moral caliber, but that the *appearance* of impropriety was something that the nonprofit wanted to avoid. In the end, the board stood with her, the matter was settled with an agreement that contained Confidentiality and Non-Admission clauses and all was quickly put behind them. Leah emptied her retirement account.

Overeager children, noses pressed to panes, watched as the first flakes of snow fell on Crow Station, Kentucky. Windows fogged with excited wintergreen breath. A salting like sequins glittered in the light from flickering streetlamps that lined the empty streets. Brother hugged sister, cousin clutched cousin, dogs bayed and cats darted beneath guest-bed dust ruffles. Teeth chattered in heads and down on the already workweek-weary masses, snow snowed. On the television the attractive newspeople smiled. Eager meteorologists capered before swirling images in bright colors, gesticulating at shapes that they could not themselves see, intoning, all shirtsleeves and perspiration, *Three inches, five inches, eight inches to accumulate. The temperature keeps dropping, no bottom in sight.* Their eyes flickered with joy.

Everything would be closed come morning. Schools closed and warehouses emptied and stores shuttered. Only the faint glow emitted by the tanning parlors that lined Fourth Street remained—bronzed attendants sitting idly behind the counter, listening to the crackling radio, flipping through months-old magazines. The storm shouldn't have been a surprise to anyone as bunions and hunting accidents across Harrod County had felt this coming for months.

In the grocery store, people filled carts with marshmallows, Vienna sausages, hair barrettes, beets, taco shells, T-bones, antibacterial wipes, baby lotion, spice drops, weightlifting magazines, garlic salt, condoms, and processed cheeses of every sort. All fled the shelves clasped in eager hands desperate to provide for their family at nearly any cost. Gloved knuckles clutched extra-large store-brand bottles of ginger ale. Faces formed fists and eyes were squinted against the profane selfishness of everyone else. Near the deli, the voices of overwhelmed babies rang, swamping the *Feel Good Hits of the Seventies, Eighties, Nineties and Today!* sputtering from aged cloth-covered speakers. Godly fathers raised their voices at elderly women, their faces red from bellowing. Spittle rained. As they reached for the movie-butter flavored popcorn on the top shelf, the scapulae of women, thin from smoking, moved like the mandibles of great wasps. Children yanked each other's ducktails and tore open the packages of cheap plastic toys so they could put them in their mouths. Leah Shepherd wandered around the deli and checked her cell phone to see if there was a message. There wasn't. A hum of desperation flocked up from the throats of the now sweating throng. Outside, cars sat motionless against one another and honked half-heartedly. By nine, the night was deep and the waning crescent moon's face was lost behind the charged quilt overhead. A pitiful sliver of silver.

The next morning, there was a thick coat of white on everything like a caul of fat. The air was crisp with silence. Children slept in. Parents slept in. Cats, stupefied, stood on hind legs to peer out windows at the alien world. When families finally rose, they ate scrambled eggs and bacon, drank chocolate milk, and the young ran out to ruin the pristine blankness, only to return a little later, panting and red-cheeked, bored already.

On the second day after the snowstorm, a blue VW was found on the side of a country road covered in snow. The town towed the car and no one ever cared to claim it.

"Leah! Leeeeaaaaah!"

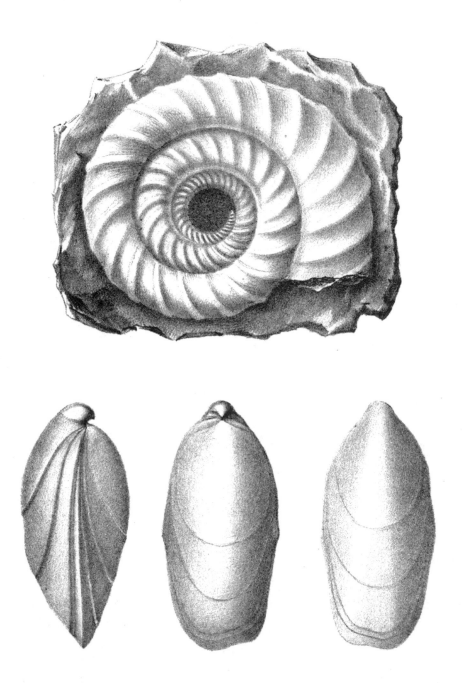

AND SO ON A FRIDAY AT THE FIRST YAWN OF summer, the sun weeps pale light on unstill children. The streets and avenues and cul de sacs and lanes swell with shouts.

Summer comes to Kentucky as a shock, as though it was impossible for the land to ever be green and full again. Magnolias with swollen white petals sway in warm breezes, record-high humid air fills lungs like warm water and the invisible mechanism that animates everything slows as summer's heavy thumb rests on its ancient belts.

Growing grass grows. Crying children cry. Dying butterflies die. Noon news warns of overheated elderly falling like flies, dehydrated bodies tumbling from lawn chairs to baking brick. Those without air conditioning wipe their necks with rags to keep beads of sweat from ruining their good clothes.

Bored children pile into the back-backs of station wagons, wearing only cut-off shorts and blue Wildcat t-shirts, and are toted out to the swimming pool, a cement bowl filled with chlorinated water and urine. They dive in head first, splash in and out, shiver with raised gooseflesh as they race to the snack bar when the lifeguard blows a rest break. One boy falls and skins his knees and cries for his mother as a young woman watches with her heart aching to see the boy's strange face. Wet lips consume frozen candy bars and cokes. The pool is a blue eye in the midst of yellow-green yards and fields that stretch out as far as anyone can tell.

Without the bonds of school, they pour out of doors, unable

to be constrained. The classroom is a coffin and the bedroom is a coffin and even their own bodies are coffins and they must escape. They climb fences and cross cow pastures in cawing gaggles, boys and girls panting, and in strings they follow the stream's muddy edges and climb embankments, passing green glass bottles half-entombed in dried mud, old newspapers with ruined words that may have once described some terrible tragedy, ripped clothes left to the rain in the tangle of a tree's old roots, and abandoned cars with trees growing through them. They follow thin tributaries off into dark bowers of bent branches and debris left by last summer's young. Boys look at the bare legs of girls who look at the bare legs of girls who look at the bare legs of boys who look at the bare legs of boys and so forth in the warm shade of dark green leaves. A shoe and a pair of underpants caught on a rock in the water as the current improvises eddies.

Still deeper, still darker, where the air is cooler, wandering farther each summer than they had the previous, unsure whom they might meet there sitting on a low branch, waiting—the ghost of some long-lost classmate, rumored to haunt the third floor girls' bathroom, foolish fire, undine and goblin, some creature that their parents warned came for bad children with glistening throat and fur matted with gore. They are too old for such things and they laugh, but they listen.

Beyond these pastures, beyond the streams and lakes, they find the remains of the Old Country Club. The Old Country Club never changes, only the children lazing in its shadows. It had been abandoned decades before even their grandparents were born, after a fire raged through a formal dance. The memory passed down of orange flames licking rafters, of embers of tulle held aloft on updrafts, of the dining hall ablaze as the young men and women pressed against the glass. The stories all agreed: Arson for sure. Lovestruck, a handsome young man with nice teeth had been put to trial and then to death and then interred somewhere forgotten. The coarse ghosts of the structure remained. Their parents and grandparents had done just as they had—clamored across rock walls and expanses of clover and knotty weeds and they thought they were the only ones who knew the Old Country Club's secrets. The youth cluster along the edge of the empty pool, gazing down into the decades of ruin and wrack. They read the collected graffiti of the county writ on the walls in red and green spray paint, find sun-bleached beer cans and exhausted condoms. Into each other's ears they whisper, lips tickling lobes. Wintergreen breath against helix and antihelix. A hand on a bare thigh. A bare neck stretched to the warmth of the sunlight. The first blush of sweat on a shoulder or stomach. Mouths on mouths around the side of the building as a boombox distant plays or behind half-crumbled slave walls, in the taller grass, with pants pulled down and arms unsure where to go, two find a moment to press into each other and in the process, lose a sock. The sun above them refuses to move. If they don't run and scream, moss and lichens will cover them and they will be pulled down into the mud, sinking away forever but the mud would be cool on the baked skin, so perhaps that fate is not so terrible.

Kentucky's air in the summer smells like dissolved and evaporated limestone. And manure, always manure. The children catch glimpses of each other's waists and knees to the sound of cassettes rewinding in cassette players because everyone wanted to hear that one song again, but the batteries are dying and everything is slowing. A medicine bottle filled with mother's cooking sherry passes from lips to lips and each partake.

Thunderstorms roll in and they run back home along the gray cement of the empty streets with the black anvils hovering behind, a billowing armada trembling with electricity. Lightning cracks and the air turns orange. Even the nights are hot, with windows open and fans a blur, the desire to stick your fingers between the bars guarding the spinning blades inexplicably strong. It is impossible to sleep in such heat, the body turning and twisting and tacky with sweat, so everyone stays up all night, listening to the chorus of crickets sounding the depth of the dark. And every night is every night that ever was all at once and every lonely boy prone in his bed is every lonely girl prone in hers, chests heaving with that painful pressure of hoping that there is someone out there unable to sleep on their account. The thunder ends. The crickets quiet. The houses settle and the only sound left is heavy breath in the night air. They get up, walk to the window and stare out at the dark yard, shallow breaths catching as they watch the shifting shape of the shadows, but it was nothing, they are certain, nothing but breeze, nothing, they are certain.

The door to the shelter was steel with reinforced glass windows. Inside, children sat in the play room, reading or watching each other play videogames on the Nintendo 64. Toys with missing legs and tangled hair slumped in the corner. College students read well-worn books to a pile of kids on the couch, as Leah Shepherd waited to meet with a mother. Because the woman had been physically abused by the father of her son, when she and her child were evicted from their two-bedroom apartment in a crumbling building downtown, she qualified for this shelter. The shelter was filled to capacity and gave priority to women who were the victims of domestic violence and likely, had the father of her children not abused her, she would have been sleeping in a car with her boy.

The boy liked to flop on the floor and kick his mother's shins and she would say, "Honey, honey, honey," and he would just kick and kick. Another mother sat in her room all day and only wanted to teach her son math and spelling above his grade while he cries to go outside. She wept when he got a problem wrong.

He hit her in the face. Leah waited and a little girl asks her if she knew any stories and Leah said, "Oh yes. I know lots of stories." Leah listened to two mothers in the hallway, out of sight, talking in rustling sounds, like leaves on a curb as a car drives past. The little girl asked Leah if she knew a story about the ghost that haunted the elementary school, but Leah said that she didn't.

The man walked toward the table where Leah was eating lunch. She looked up, but could not see his face for the midday sun streaming through the windows behind him and then he spoke her name.

Denim jacket and pegged jeans and suede boots and with a cherry taste in her mouth, the woman waited for Leah to call her into the conference room. Her cell phone clamored in tiny pearls of need. The boy's daddy had wrecked her again and she was done. Done with him and his family. Done with the calls. Done with him laying hands on her. Done with crying on the cell phone with her mother. Done with the boy looking at her from under his bed. She looked into her hands and waited for someone to respond.

A small cake crouched before them, crowned with three flickering candles. Blue candles with orange flames and tiny rivers of clear wax running down toward the white icing. "Come on, try," Mrs. Shepherd said, but Leah held firm in her refusal to blow out the candles. Her gray eyes flickered and her short arms were wrapped tight around her chest. Her mother pursed her lips, blew and the hot tongues danced and were gone.

Mrs. Shepherd cut a slice from the cake and set it in front of the now smiling girl, who promptly crammed it in her mouth with chubby paws. Mrs. Shepherd washed her daughter's hands and let her feel the thing moving in her stomach. "That's your brother," Mrs. Shepherd said and Leah made a face, wriggled free and thundered after the cat.

Leah could only remember this about Jacob's birth: the golden rectangle of her door, her father lifting her out of bed, her mother in a maroon coat that drug the ground, the razors of light from the bright fluorescents in the hospital waiting room, the smell of cigarette smoke and the voices of men and then the wailing red boy that made her clap her hands to her ears. There was more that she might have remembered, but she was certain that the rest were not her own memories, but were the creation of the pictures her mother kept around the house, in the worn albums, in boxes in her parents' bedroom. Perhaps she'd had memories of her own, but they'd been crowded out by the symphony of photographs her mother maintained. There was a time, when she was in high school and going through a phase she found unpleasant to think about now, when she would sneak into her parents' bedroom and take one of the pictures from the dozen that were laying out and then listen to her mother and father arguing, her mother accusing her father of having moved it, having moved it and forgotten where it was. Later, Leah would put it back where it had been, but her parents reconciliation and apologies, whatever they were like, were always far too quiet for her to hear.

Leah did not like to think about what she'd been like when she was younger. In fifth grade, she'd been the butt of her classmates' taunts and she'd become a terror herself, passing the pitiless jibes along. An overweight boy once tried to tease her, turning in his seat to hurl half-hearted slurs while the teacher stepped out of the classroom for a moment, a boy that Leah realized only in retrospect probably had a crush on her and was merely seeking her attention in the only way he understood. She'd mocked him without mercy. His belly poking out from under his thin shirt. The moles on his face. His cheap shoes that his parents probably bought for him used. Those sitting around them laughed and encouraged by their laughter, by being on this side of their laughter, Leah kept on until the boy filled the room with the slurp of his half-stifled sobs. The next day, the boy's parents called the school to report the bullying and the school called the Shepherds and Mr. Shepherd sat his daughter down that afternoon and asked her why she would do such a thing. Say the things the principal told him she'd said. Leah shrugged, unsure. "I've never been more ashamed." Looking back, Leah wished that she could say that it had been a moment that had changed her. That she'd become the boy's defender after that, protecting him against the older children who call the boys far worse things. That they'd become close friends and stayed that way through the years and grades. She stopped taunting the boy in class only because she didn't want to get in trouble with her parents, but she turned her torment elsewhere. She would have done anything to keep the other children from turning back on her.

Leah tried not to think about those years and how terrible she'd been. She hoped that some of the things she'd said were no longer remembered by anyone.

The babysitter said, "Come here," and Leah came and sat down next to her on the floor. "Listen. Do you want to hear something terrible?" The babysitter was only five years older than Leah, but seems to be from another generation. She wore pale pink shorts over pool-tanned legs, green flip-flops on long-toed feet, a soft blue t-shirt on broad swimmer's shoulders. Her braces gleamed.

"Listen to this. So at the lake once, I was swimming. This was a few summers ago. My parents have a place there they rent in the summer. It's like a log cabin and there is a fireplace in the middle of the living room and we toast marshmallows, but mine always burn and get all mushy and stuff, but so, we were at the lake a few summers ago and I was swimming and I wanted to see how far out I could swim. My mom and step-dad were on the dock in folding chairs and my older brother was away with some of his friends from college or something and I was swimming alone because, see, I wanted to see if I could swim out to this thing I saw floating out in the water. It was a buoy or something, so I swam the breaststroke, because I'd just learned that for the swim team and I wanted to practice. The lake is wide there, before the last turn before the dam, so it was real far, but I wanted to make it, so I kept moving my arms and kicking. Then I got to the thing and I put my hand out and it turned and I could see that it was a person's head and half was covered in moss and stuff and the other half was bloated and pale and green and the eyes had worms in them. I found out later that it was a guy who'd been in a boating accident."

When you swim in the lake, strapped into your life-vest, you bob in brown-green water. You dangle over endless murk. Branches, you hope, brush your ankles. Pale shapes pass beneath you, just out of the range of vision, obscure submerged glaciers of alien fish flesh or some larking phantom. The lake is man-made. At the bottom of the lake, there were houses. Her father told her so. When you swim in the lake, slipping out of your life-vest for a moment, to dart down to the sudden cold strata of water just out of range of the sun, you are on the threshold of a frightening and serene city unseen by anyone still living, but at home, when dry and warm, you can taste that empty city in every sip of water you take from the tap.

The babysitter said, "You believe me, don't you?" and Leah nodded and the babysitter said, "Have I ever told you that my house is haunted?"

Jacob cried and beat fists on air to follow Leah as she darted out the door to find the neighborhood boys who play football in the street on Saturday mornings. They played football in the middle of the street and threw firecrackers at passing cars and tried to knock each other off of their bicycles with bull whips purchased at the Harrod County Fair.

Sometimes the neighborhood boys let her play, but not if Jacob came. They called him names and he cried and the boys scattered in guffaws. She got angry that they wouldn't let her play and that Jacob ruined it for her and felt terribly alone as they sauntered away, their throats full of laughter like a skull full of honey.

The neighborhood boys were much older. Two were in middle school and one could even drive a car already, or said he could. They yelled in the early summer evening and Leah could hear them from her window. They made fun of her too when she tagged along, nipping at their shadows, but she didn't mind as long as they didn't turn away from her. Their voices sliced summer's monotony.

Leah couldn't find the boys. They were not in the street. They were not at the house with the walled garden and the reflecting pool. They were not behind the house abutting the empty lot. She could hear voices somewhere, but it might have been just a radio in a passing car. She knew they were somewhere on the street. She tilted up her ears and listened for them.

Somewhere, they pitched rocks, called names, cursed soft

curses to each other. Their faces glistened in the sunlight and eyes flamed at the words cock pussy slut balls titties shit motherfucker shit shit.

An egg, hidden and forgotten at Easter, started to smell. *The Devil is in my closet.* Leah curled in the corner of her bed, staring at the closet door. When she went to the bathroom to bathe before bed, the door had been closed. When she returned, it was open. In the dark, she could feel cold air blowing against her face like faint breath. She'd been a bad sister and this was her punishment. The Devil and Hell and pain for ever and ever. A voice called her name from the closet. A voice whispered *help.*

At school, she had no friends. Her round face and her wiry hair and her slightly too small eyes and her stooping gait conspired to leave her outside the circle of voices on the playground. The school year passed and she had little that she remembered about it later on except for the TRS-80 computer that the school put in the library, on which she played simple games, green lines on a black field. And then a summer passed and a school year passed and still, little happened to her that she would remember. On the playground during recess, sitting alone, she carved her name into the wood of the log cabin with a pair of scissors that she'd spirited out in her skirt. Pale letters in dark, wet wood. Her purchase of eternity.

One evening as she left work, Leah Shepherd wondered if her name was still there, carved in the wood of the playground of the old elementary school. She parked on the street and started across the school yard toward the playground, but seeing a group of children playing unsupervised after school, she felt uncomfortable and left. They watched her go and laughed from the top of the jungle gym.

"Between her legs. Lots of bald heads been there," he said and laughed. He pulled his shirt up and picked at tangled hairs. He'd replaced his eyes with marbles and his teeth with gravel. He shot at the sky and night died finding the Earth new in new light.

She just needed a little help until her job started paying. Leah listened to her story, signed papers and watching the woman walk outside the conference room window, she lost the train of conversation.

Thin sticks found on the ground after thunderstorms were the scourge of summer. Her clothes scattered among the roots and rocks. She took cover under an overpass. The phloem and xylem inside still tender. Rough bark abrading young skin. Still tender. Still young. Young gods die young. The palace beyond this world rotting even as it is born. Young die young. Accumulate, fade, emptiness and an evening of rain with no thunder. Just static. A woman gathered her clothes when it was over, after the man had gone, leaving behind a cloud of his breath, her clothes dried on the cement.

Leah was startled by the telephone's trill and the voice that came with it, asking for just a little help and Leah looked deep into the spreadsheets to find it.

Leah couldn't remember when she first saw the man. In her earliest memory of him, something which barely even counted as a memory, something which was little more than a faintly colored feeling, something without image or sound or words to describe it, an electrical impulse that rushed through her mind that she might call a memory, but which was some more elemental and ancient relative, some sooty palm print on a cave wall, in this she remembered *recognizing* him, which means that she'd seen him before, but she could not remember when or from where. This is how it was when she, in bed in the dark, sought her earliest impressions, nested in the most distant fold of her memory, something inconsequential—putting on a shoe on a step or the muted swirls in the tarnished silver of the hutch in the dining room—but there was always a day before that that she had lived and the sense that there was a whole world and life just beyond. She had the same feeling when she read the Book of Genesis. There is always something that came before, something forgotten. Fragments reflecting some earlier tale, now long lost. In bed she sought those old shards, suffocated under years of non-profit tax regulations and names of acquaintances and television episodes, and when she thought of that man, she wondered if she'd really seen anyone at all.

Edna L. Toliver Elementary School was bounded by city streets on three sides. Beyond the street that ran behind the school, warehouses and then beyond, train tracks. It was the fall. There was nothing remarkable about this man, walking along the edge of the property. An adult, but how old was unknown to her. Tall with a slight gut that strained against whatever shirt he wore, or was hidden under a jacket of one sort or another. A gut, but thin looking. Thin arms swinging like a skeleton dancing in a cartoon. His hair was brown or black, and sometimes, in the right light had blond highlights and was slightly gray in places and with thick framed glasses.

The first time, she just looked up and noticed the man walking along the street behind the school slowly. He became singular in her mind as though God had paused the rest of the world and said, *Look*. After that, she saw him everywhere. Walking behind or next to the school, in department stores or outside of church, cutting through the old church cemetery next to the sanctuary, leaning against the obelisk, loafing on the steps of an apartment or entering the dark doorway of a pool hall. Sometimes he looks a little different, seemed to stand straighter or stoop. Seemed to lose and gain weight. Maybe he began to dye his hair. He sometimes wore glasses. And she only saw the man when Jacob was around. Only when Jacob careened around the playground, only when he tottered out of her reach, only then would Leah notice the man standing off in the distance or walking with his face turned away. She watched the man, her neck growing warm, birds swirling in the young sky.

"I don't know how you work at a place like that. I'd get sick of all the stories. The excuses you know? These girls, they get in trouble and then they expect someone else to take care of their problems. You know? I mean, I know sometimes people need help, but when you keep having babies and you've got a cell phone and you're texting and updating your status and shit, you know? I don't know how you do it. But, I mean, it's a good thing, but some people abuse it."

That evening, over a meal, the solicitation for a donation was already forgotten.

"Leah," Jacob said, looking out the window when they were supposed to be asleep. "Leah."

"Don't tell me there is someone in the yard because there's not."

"Okay," Jacob said and giggled.

Can I love these children? Mrs. Shepherd wondered once while watching them run in the dry summer grass as she sipped iced tea from a plastic cup. The screaming and crying, the falling and bloody knees, the soiled pants and ruined mattresses, the death of any hope of just a moment of quiet as the two cannoned through the halls. *Go outside! Go outside! Please, Christ Jesus, go outside!* She kept an anthology of poetry from her freshman year of college in a drawer by her bed and would open it once in a while and read a few poems, always opening to the same places where the spine was broken, wondering why she underlined certain lines. When she was first pregnant with Leah, Mrs. Shepherd stopped working and didn't go back to work until Leah was in high school. She got a realtor's license and within a few years was making far more than her husband made as a public school teacher and administrator. They were comfortable. She lost the anthology in one of their moves.

At night, Mr. Shepherd embraced his wife and told her he loved her and she smiled to make him feel better, as though there was nothing wrong with them, nothing wrong with her, and she waited for him to let her go.

Can I love these children?

Standing at the window in the kitchen, putting away the old plastic cups that the family used for years, the lips chewed and uncomfortable now, she remembers having wondered that once and watched as the cups fell to the kitchen floor, slipping from her fingers.

Mr. Shepherd took his children to a matinee. Windows open in the car to spring air and there were new leaves on old trees. Backlit by early afternoon sun they gleamed light green. Jacob pointed out his favorite tree, a telephone pole by the elementary school. With a scab on his nose, he sat still and watched out the window, hoping to see a blue Bug. His hair, bleached on accident by their mother, swarmed his ears. Dashboard speakers crackled with the thud of drums. They thrilled. Leah stretched out across the back, her bare legs sticking to ripped vinyl seats spilling foam. An empty blue sky ribboned out behind the houses and water-towers. Windows sheared off sheets of the warm spring air and it spilled across her face. They walked into the dark of the theater. They were late. The movie had begun. They sat in the back row.

A ship on fire. A black horse's head struggling against the black water. A boy on a beach. Yellow sun shining on him, hotter than it had on us. The boy does not speak. They run. They rest. They are alone.

The theater was full of other children. Ragged edges of their heads lit by the screen. They flickered. Though no sound came from the boy or the horse on the screen, a soft wordless flutter rose from the seats. Squeaks and moans, heavy throated laughs. Leah and Jacob sit in silence and watch the movie and listen to the other children.

The boy and horse flying across dunes, a mud yellow fort on the horizon, the sun setting, endless rays.

Later: "We saw a green fire and a whale and a skeleton and a person with two heads and a raccoon that was standing and screaming…" Nighttime and the windows exploded with rippling light. The squall without dim compared to the bellowing within from startled children pressing faces to plaster. A bending outside, a quaking of cracking, an impossibly deep sound that Leah assumed could only be the Earth being ripped in two.

The next morning, the children marveled at the limb that had crushed the car. "We could have been in there," Jacob said, astonished at his luck. The shards found thereafter, saved for years, glinting bits slicing at bare toe, placed by Leah in a nook in magnolia roots as a reminder of their luck. Waves beat bones of crawling things to sand and dust and compress to limestone teeth that jut from the green jaw of green grass. Sea-shattered remnant and so too will these baby bones be. And here they are now, in the palm of Leah's hand and hidden in her yard. Jacob asked for the pretty pieces and Leah said no because they were her shards. Years of glass.

"I don't want to! I don't want to go!" Jacob screwed his red face and beat white fists at empty air. Baby blue pleated shorts and slate blue sport coat and red tie. He hopped and gesticulated, face puffed-up like a scarlet balloon. "I'll run away!" Where the cement cracked and brown sprigs of grass jutted up through, he stood, screamed and screamed, a high pitched voice ricocheting around the empty curves of St. Mildred's Court, a voice that Leah was certain could be heard through all of Crow Station. He pitched a teary tantrum and his sister pleaded with him to not run away, which he threatened every Sunday when told it was time for church. No cars drove past. The deaf man across the street was not mowing. The world contained only the two of them, brother and sister, alone in the world, still but for the rustling of the spring's newly born leaves in the branches of the ancient trees that bent over them, the only living things listening to them. "No, no. Please, don't. Don't. I will let you sleep in the bed by the door. I will give you a back scratch every night. I will pick up your toys."

"All of them?"

"Yes."

"How long?"

"A week." He began to walk away. "Okay, a month." He came home.

"Hell, no. That house ain't haunted. That's bullshit, but look, someone does live there. I mean I've seen him. A real small fellow. We were out with Jason and them and he wanted to see it, so we drove by and up the long drive to the door and Jason and his cousin were going to go in, but when we stopped the front door opened up and this little guy comes running out at the car and well, we just fucking booked it, and the guy was screaming and screaming and I looked back and he followed us most of the way down the street."

Cherry and cinnamon exhalations and the coming evening quilted quiet stars over the courthouse as the custody hearing went longer than expected.

Children swam, gradually threading out into murky water to murky depths. Mothers in tank-tops leaned against cushions, sunglasses dull. Books with broken spines and books with swollen pages. Yellow edges and black blooms and a warm smell. Dead-leaf grot on lofts of lake water. Blue between branches dimmed. The mothers dozed and across the lake a filthy-looking woman walked through the trees, looking down at the children between the trunks, far from the bare arms of the sunlight. Without fear, the children dared one another to swim out across the water's skin, out to the drain pipe that runs under the road, to swim through. On the other side, a stream, smooth rocks, water lapping air, muddy bank slipping green into clear water. They extended arms beyond the prickly blue rope, the freedom of the whole lake just beyond. One was missing, so they called and listened for his response. They sounded games, eyes closed, arms aflail, searching for the missing body, screaming and grabbing but not finding. They called and called, listening for that voice in response, that splash, imagining, eyes closed, diving down to the bottom of the man-made lake, the sunken plain, the abandoned homes still standing empty below them. They found him and it was someone else's turn to go missing. Across the water, where the branches overhang, dead leaves lapped at spinning green water.

"Honey, don't worry so much. Your brother isn't going to run away. Your father won't let anything happen. He is just throwing a fit because he doesn't like to wear a tie. Ignore him and he'll stop. Please."

The neighborhood boys who liked to push little children down. The boys who curse and call names. The boys who ask what sex is and laugh when you blush. The girls who call names and squirt white glue into your hair on lice-check day. The girls who bite and roll their eyes. The boys and girls screaming and swirling around the playground. The girls and boys pushing and pulling and pinching and touching and smelling of dried drool.

Perched on the top of the jungle gym, she watched Jacob sitting alone near the other children his grade on rotting railroad ties. Her classmates whispered to her about this one boy who—

And they giggled. The bell trilled. The children flocked in.

And at night she sat on the edge of Jacob's bed, crawling over in the dark after he pestered her for several minutes for a story and she told him about the boy who was bad and got lost in the woods and heard something following him on the path, something large, something growling and breathing, something that smelled like the wet leaves underneath of the dry leaves. Something that smelled like blood and they both got a little scared at that even though neither knew what blood smelled like.

Perhaps the wind blows through the branches of the maples like a breeze through nails. The boy met the Devil, whose real name is Christopher Lark. Leah described his bloody teeth and yellow eyes and the terrible awful breath that smelled like mushrooms. When she noticed that Jacob was terrified, she stopped the story and told him that she was just making stuff up and kissed him on the forehead but she could feel him shivering. She looked at Jacob in the dark and the bright shadows passed and they lost count of the shapes and sounds. If the car passed to the right, Jacob got a point and if it passed to the left, Leah did. Jacob asked who was winning and she didn't know because she lost count when he got ahead. He asked how many stars there were and she didn't know that either.

All children want to go to space. Earth only offers parents wailing about overdraft notices and evening news playing in an empty den. Dead pets too. Childhood is a rot. And so they look up and see stars shiver, ancient information only just now arriving, because that is the only place left to look, and they yearn. The Earth crumbles back into itself but there, spinning space stations, eternal bulbs of light, children, unaware of their parents calling them from the screened-in porch, lie on their backs on hillsides, razor blades of grass pricking them through their shirts, their eyes on the black mesh above them, the white pin pricks in the fabric, like a lovely city seen from above.

The young child jabbered and wailed along the crumbling brick walk. The tongues of paper, the limbs in last light, the dark halls of the empty church unexplored. In the department store, Leah waited by the bank of windows for her turn to pay as the growing mass, shivering and thrumming, cackled into palms or stared down into pixilated stigmata. Women in coats, puffy with down, colors faded, dirty faux-fur trim. Women in faded jeans, in sweatpants, in nice slacks. Women in hoodies and in blouses their mothers gave them. Women in clothes from mothers and aunts and church drives. Women in ill-fitting clothes purchased at Goodwill. Nice suits on strong shoulders. Nice shirts over swell of breast and swell of stomach and swell of hips. Over thin arms and thin shoulders. Bare shoulders. Rasping, singing, calling, drawling. The smell of shampoo and hair and bodies and breath and perfume and deodorant and cigarettes and cough cough cough. The children sit and stare or ramble. The cell phones toll tones, squawk messages, titter and trill. One moment, a glance, one second, thumbs trembling, a sigh, a laugh, do you mind, one moment, a grunt, a moan, and "See, see? This is what I mean."

And out the window, across the parking lot, along the road, in the glitter of glints of sunlight off of passing cars, that filthy woman was walking, her long brown hair hanging in greasy vines, and despite the distance, Leah felt certain that she could clearly see the woman's face, the thick black liner around eyes that were fixed straight ahead as she walked. Her cheeks rouged and a glimmer of something like earrings seen momentarily in the gaps of her swaying hair. And then she passed beyond the edge of the window and Leah, next in line, had to turn to the dark of the cash register and complete her transaction.

In her apartment, she wondered what it would be like to wander in the woods by the stream alone, in the dark, but went to sleep instead.

"At night he turns into a snake and comes and taps on my window." The children gather around Leah when she visited the shelter, begging for her to play. One boy whispered in her ear and Leah looked at him confused. One girl asked Leah if she was white and Leah felt embarrassed to answer. The boy told the little girl, as they sat next to Leah, that he could "see him outside at night."

Listen: The rooms are cool. Moss reminds her of home. A gale of smoke. They pushed up the nails and her heart stopped. She carved *our place* into the banister. Listen: Sun teeming on warm grass. Glassy rays. A dogwood, the bloody crowns, maple and magnolia. At night she would press her hands into her eyes as she lay in her bed and watch the phosphorescent blips recede into the milky black. She knew her name would be gone if she looked. *See how high I can climb?* The stream eddied and her eyes went slack. Listen: Daylight walls dun colored, carpets crème, halls mint, ceiling eggshell. Tiles sagging from rainwater. Plaster buckling from rainwater. At night all blue-black nothing. Already going gray. Thick wrists and hands. Far from attractive. Watery blood dried quick around the nails. *Look at me.* Listen: A pawing at the window. *Look.* Listen: The girl drew a boy with a city behind him, a farmhouse and grapes under ground. A man on a hill clawing the sun. Rays dripping down his arms in gold and silver. *Leah!* Listen: A rake's gaze at the lazy girls, drying themselves off. *Leeaaah!* Listen: A cracked blue egg. The edges of the field, lined with tobacco or corn or dead rot disappear over the full-bellied knoll. Or warehouses blown down. Or houses burned. Or barns falling in from the wheeling of seasons. From an odd spot above, see the little boy running deeper. The stalks sulking, the Easter best, a last swish of sun-bleached hair and then he slips below the surface like a coin into a fountain, his shadow more than enough to set off a commotion of brightly shaped flashes in the front of his sister's eyes. His mother calls and calls from a porch, painted Passover pink. Leah never remembered these evenings, even as they took more and more of her time, though she often had thoughts of large white machines, smooth, flowing lines of lights.

Wake, wake! It is time for work, will you children never listen? And the stream too ruined by rain to see her face in any longer. She dialed John Rhodes' cell phone number.

In the hyper-clear sky hung the moon and Orion in full. A splash of pale light, the swirling disc of their galaxy, the arms of an octopus. She tallied for her brother the stars of all of the constellations, named and unnamed, known and forgotten and not yet charted. The stars don't know their own names. The constellations can't see what shape they are. Leah sat in the window of their bedroom and looking out, named them for Jacob. The black dome of the void centered above their house on the corner of the street where thin dry grass juts through cracks in the sidewalk and sun-bleached bottle caps and broken glass from old wrecks rests.

Communion trays ready to be taken to the shut-ins. The broken body and spilled blood. The small white tiles of bread and plastic cups of grape juice. Leah opened the car door, lifted the tray, walked to the house and knocked on the screen. When they were growing up, Leah and Jacob would go with their mother to take communion to the shut-ins. Leah hated it. She felt uncomfortable around the old women. They were all women. She was scared to see them curled in their beds, thin, trapped between bed sheets, mouths open, moaning, eyes unseeing, the smell of urine and bodies and cleaning fluid, the women curling up like a dried leaf, but Mrs. Shepherd took her children with her because they were doing an Important Thing. Jacob would go right up to the women and if they were awake, if they called out to him, called a name of a son in some other state, he would answer and they would reach out and he would take their hand. But Leah would linger by the door and wait. Knobs of spine through a nightgown. A papery voice asking her name.

Leah called the old woman's name and waited a moment before she walked in. A morning and the moon still clung to life like a crescent cloud. Some things are just for the night. Leah called her name, carrying communion. For how many years did she bring communion to the wrecked rooms? The stale bed? Still when Leah took communion to the church's shut-in members, she dreaded it for the week leading up to Sunday. But she did it and the old woman in the house she'd come to enjoy being around and Leah would visit her on other days, just to sit and talk, or sit and look out at the evening coming on.

She called out to the old woman and saw the light on in the basement.

After the suit was filed, Leah had a meeting with Judge James Whitehead (retired). The judge had been on the board of directors of the nonprofit since his retirement and had been one of its founders years before. The judge had known Leah for a very long time, since before he was appointed to the bench. When he'd been in private practice, he'd represented the Shepherd family on a number of matters, beginning with defending Mr. Shepherd when he was charged with the assault and battery of a Sunday school teacher.

"Leah," the judge said as she walked in. She began to say something to defend herself, but he waved his hands emphatically, a gesture the local bar had learned meant *You should be quiet now* and said, "None of this means a pinch of puppy shit. Their attorney is a moth-eaten gasbag out for a fee, but, listen, we have to get this settled now. I am behind you because I know you and I will go to bat for you, but the board is skittish." Leah was looking out the window of his office at the Crow Station skyline. On the office stereo, she could hear a Tallis motet. The judge smelled like cough drops. He smiled at her and she felt, for a moment, that it would, in the end, be okay.

Despite the three years between them, Leah and Jacob Shepherd were rippling reflections of one another. Soft round faces and short unruly hair and cheeks quick to turn red when bodies darted and whirled. Their throats wailed the same strong wails when angry and their hearts beat the same rapid beats when winded from their running and when bad, their lips turned into the same red comma. Capering across limestone, slipping down mossy bank, slipping, skittering, spilling down green, smearing green on knees, drawing red, all four knees, both of them capering, they were the same, Jacob only a smaller version of his sister. Refractions split by facets. One in two places, bilocated, capering and splashing and yelping. In public, passing parents *tsked* at these bad children.

Mrs. Shepherd wanted Leah to grow her hair out, but whenever it began to tickle her neck, Leah would sneak into her parents' bedroom and take the scissors, or if they were hidden, she would slip into the kitchen and take a butcher knife, and chop chunks of it away, leaving irregular whorls of brown wherever they fell. Her brother didn't have this problem as no one ever commented on his hair, leaving him to decide how he wanted it, yet he always cut it to match his sister's hair. "Why do you do this?" Mrs. Shepherd would ask. "You have such lovely hair. You would be so beautiful if you would let it grow out." She said this as she smacked the girl across the backs of her thighs. Leah raised red, wet eyes, a sore backside, and slithered to her room to sulk and moan. *You could have been so beautiful.*

Their skin, a map bruised and scratched. Complimentary rivers of red and bays of black. She could see their blue veins under their skin. They looked like letters that she tried to read. Four hazel eyes between the two of them. She would make Jacob sit in the light, eyes wide so she could look into them. She wanted to see how the iris was made. A gray honeycomb in a glass dome.

The black bands and the gray iris spiraling around the blackest holes. Light swallowed up. Their eyes looked like the surface of the lake. Eye lashes were bent bare branches. Tears were rain overrunning creek beds.

Constellations of freckles across nose and cheek and the back of necks. When she lay in bed, waning daylight slanting in, he would lean over her and draw his finger across the freckles, connecting them in figures and explaining to her their meaning. *You could have been.*

The woman said her father was an orthodontist with thick forearms and for her birthday he gave her a leather-bound notebook which she planned to use to write a fantasy story about a strange land of strange animals and strange people, but her parents were yelling and the house was dark and she was downstairs and a door was battering its frame and the moon was too loud in the room. One morning, while her parents were sleeping, she slipped out the door of the house in the gray light of an empty Sunday morning and floated along the street away from there.

The receptionist, a woman who had to kick out one young tenant because she found out that the young tenant had taken some of the receptionist's pain killers, smiled and nodded.

When Leah came in, the receptionist, an older woman who moved through space as though she'd never not been beautiful, said, "I'm sorry if this is a personal question, but—" then the telephone rang and Leah went to her office and the receptionist, who'd once dated a doctor, decades ago, who never would leave his wife, never asked the question.

———————

"This girl in my church, she had this demon that was in her and it would make her fall down during service and roll and the preacher would lay hands and after a bit she would open her eyes and start to cry. Then after church, we'd walk down to the movies and see whatever was on, or tell our parents that was what we was doing and just sneak out the backdoor and hang out behind the theater with some guys from the county school. The demon never touched her there, but from the start I knew it was a bad idea for her to go with that one guy to the haunted house and try and spend the night there. Like I say, it weren't haunted, but that's not the only bad that can happen."

At some point after the suit to challenge the Last Will and Testament of the old woman was filed, after discovery had completed and the attorneys had deposed everyone they could think of, one of the beneficiaries of the old woman's estate, the oldest son, contacted Leah Shepherd personally and proposed that they meet without their attorneys to discuss settling the case "without those lawyers eating up all our money."

They met for lunch at a chain restaurant that had just opened up on the bypass around Crow Station. Leah felt nervous because she disliked confrontation, but the man was soft-spoken, up until the moment when he, with his fat fingers, began to rub Leah's shoulders and suggested terms of the possible settlement which shocked Leah to silence. She stood and began to walk out, past a table of elderly women having a birthday party, and the man, a firmly built fifty-year-old with a shaved head who'd made a name for himself with a construction company in Indiana, called her a cunt and a whore, booming, his soft voice gone, across the mostly empty restaurant, and he swore to her that she would be sorry, for being a fucking tease and being a fucking dyke and for stealing from his sainted mother. His scalp flashed red. His floral print shirt was unbuttoned at the top and his white chest hair seemed to glow against the skin of his chest. It looked like cauliflower. He had spit on his lips and followed her out to the parking lot, barking, and he stared at her as she drove away. When she stopped at a stop light several blocks away, she looked in her rearview mirror at the chain restaurant in the distance and could see him still standing outside, a tiny speck, staring at her car.

When Jacob heard the boys on the playground making fun of Leah's birthmark, Jacob told them that they shouldn't make fun of it because she could make a creature with long claws that would come snatch them away. The boys laughed at him and ran off, jingling their change, eager for Mountain Dew and Mello Yello, for Jolt and Ale-8-One, but later, when they were at home alone, in bed, listening to the nothing of night, they sought silence through prayer and licked with their sugar sticky lips and jumped when the wind tried the windowpane.

Did Jacob ever wish that creature to come?

So each summer day when expelled from the house by their mother and father, they crept and snuck, cutting through yards and driveways, avoiding any spot that was too open, pretending they were space explorers. Once, cutting through a backyard they found a sundial in the middle of a garden. "What time is it?" Jacob asked.

"I don't know. The arm thing is broke off. Stand on it."

He clambered up, tipping the time piece and squealing, they scrambled away, never to cut through that yard again.

While his sister slept, he listened to the backdoor open and someone come up the stairs. And then voices, soft, and he slept.

The History of Lycanthropy in Europe and Asia Minor. Occult Practices of the Nazis (with 12 New Illustrations). The older girls sunned themselves in bikinis by the diving board. They whispered to each other and yelled up to the shirtless boys in the lifeguard chairs. *Chariot of the Gods. The Human Body (with 4 Color Fold-Out). Monsters You've Never Heard Of. The Encyclopedia of Monsters.* Jacob wanted to dive off of the high dive, something Leah was sure he was too young to do, but their grandmother, Mr. Shepherd's mother, was asleep under her umbrella and the lifeguards were watching the young girls saunter on hot cement, so Leah didn't tell him not to. She didn't like the pool, but enjoyed reading the books their grandmother brought her from the library where she worked. *The True History of UFOs. Stone Circles of North America and Other Unexplained Wonders. Ghostly Tales of Love and Revenge. Scary Stories to Tell in the Dark. The Severed Hand. The Girl With the Ribbon Around Her Neck and Other Folktales.* He climbed, checking to make sure Leah was still watching. He walked to the end of the blue tongue suspended in the empty sky above the blue water. He waved at her. *Curses, Hexes and Spells.* He wanted her to put aside the books and watch him, *Watch watch watch!* She turned to look up at him standing, hands on knees, gazing over the edge at the faraway water.

"Leah! Leeaaah!"

———————

A man she did not know walked up to her while she was waiting for her lunch to come and said, "Leah?" She looked up at him as he waited to be invited to sit.

"Why did your mother let them go all day at the pool with no sunscreen? Look at that burn on poor Jacob's nose." Mrs. Shepherd cooed over the burn which would eventually become covered with a scab that looked like a lost continent. Mr. Shepherd shrugged. The scab covered the burn and lasted for months and months. In Leah's memories of her brother, he always had this scab, no matter the year or season.

Mrs. Shepherd tried to lighten Jacob's hair and bleached it bone white. This is how Leah remembered him as well.

Each morning, Mrs. Shepherd woke her children by turning on the light in the bedroom and singing a hymn. One Christmas, Leah gave her brother a cheap plastic car. She told her mother that she'd saved her allowance for months and had purchased the blue car from the small rack of cheap toys in the back corner of the Convenient across the street from the elementary school one afternoon before walking home. So proud her mother was of such generosity. Those last seven months, Jacob slept with the car every night.

The first Leah could remember: They held her out over the slumping slave wall and she pointed at the cows drinking clouds out of a barrel. Her mother's legs were made of grass and her stomach out of the dirt and her breasts out of the sun and her hair out of the night. The cows licked the sky from their noses and swayed.

Leah mentioned the memory to her mother who pulled out the picture from the old photo album showing Mrs. Shepherd in green and yellow holding Jacob out to a cow in a field. Her mother smirked and put the picture back.

A gnarl of green branches and crackling leaves. Under it, the ground is bare of grass blades and always damp with mud. Bits of rock and glass found in the gutter by the storm drain. When a thunderstorm washes the crushed, colorful glass and dead leaves through the cement furrows, they flow here.

"Leah, honey, please get your hands out of that mess. You are going to prick your finger and get a blood disease or tetanus. Your jaw will lock up and you will never be able to eat again. The doctor will have to cut a hole in your throat, like one that man has who lives next to your aunt, the one with the robot voice. You will have a hole like that and you will have to eat baby food through it for the rest of your life. We will have to hire a nurse to sponge off the mucus that will grow around the hole and you will have a decaying smell about you for the rest of your life and no one will ever marry you." No one ever did marry Leah Shepherd, though she was engaged for a time during graduate school to a man named Derrick Green. The failure of their relationship had nothing to do with a blood disease or tetanus. He told a joke at a party, his lips covered in spittle as he gave the punchline and his friends roared in laughter and told him he was terrible and Leah recoiled and he saw the look of disgust on her face and he gave her a look that said, *What?* and *Oh, come on, it's just a joke.* Later, as they drove home from the party, he picked at her about her disapproval of the joke, even though she'd not said anything about it, but he'd been with her for a year and he knew that it hurt her, but he knew she would just let it fester and he wanted to get it out, to go ahead and fight so that they could move beyond it, but she wouldn't talk to him at all. "You are overreacting," he said. She didn't break off the engagement, but he could tell it was over and they eventually just ceased being a couple and it had nothing to do with broken glass.

The sizzle of its electric-lit windows and the soft, hazy waver of the horizon of glass towers and neon signs—

It was always the same: Jacob was scared and wanted to get into bed with his big sister, but he wouldn't let her sleep, wanting instead to talk all night, clutching his toy car and talking and flailing about, so Leah would tell him that if he didn't lie quiet, a monster would come for him, and then he would start to whimper and she would feel sad for having scared her little brother and then she would put a long freckled arm over Jacob and tell him that there were no monsters. No ghost or witch or vampire. No creatures clawing or baying. No secret codes or forgotten tales, whistling languages and alien photography. No God in the sky making your skin sick for saying something bad. Nothing. No monsters, no ghosts, but the man she'd seen, how could she tell her brother to be careful of him? Their father had had a talk with them about not going with strangers. She'd gone into her parents' bedroom one night and told them, "Jacob said there is a man in the backyard," but Mr. Shepherd, after looking at the glowing green arms of the clock next to the bed, said, "There is no one in the yard. You two need to go to sleep," and he rolled over on his other side. So Leah took it upon herself to fill her brother's head with a fear of anything she could, but she always felt guilty when he cried, so she backpedalled. Jacob, for his part, loved his sister, there in the burrow of dark, and he listened to her comforting words, but he didn't believe her. He'd heard someone knocking on the door in the middle of the night once. He knew better.

"Isn't it nice, Jacob. Your big sister got it for you. A little car. Say thank you, Jacob. Say thank you." Leah told her mother that she'd saved her allowance and bought the car at the Convenient across the street from the school, but Leah had actually spent her allowance on candy for herself and then stolen the small blue car, walking out of the store with it hidden in her pocket on the last day of school before Christmas break and even though the middle-aged woman behind the counter hadn't noticed Leah take the car, Leah was certain that she would be caught, that the woman would notice the car was gone and would know that she had taken it and all Christmas break Leah worried that she would get caught. Every time the telephone rang, Leah's heart leapt, sure that this was the middle-aged woman calling to tell the Shepherds that their daughter was a thief, which never happened because the woman didn't notice Leah taking the toy car, and even if she had, it was unlikely that she would have cared—they didn't pay her enough to care—yet Leah never went back to the Convenient, too full of shame and fear, and even now, three decades later, she avoided the store, the name of which was changed to Chill's Quik Stop.

They coursed through the house, up the front stairs and down the back, out the front door and around the side of the house, hands reaching out to beat at the holly bushes, the holly leaves scratching their tender palms, feet stomping earth and they bellowed and mewed at each other, howled and howled, ran past the back of the house where the porch was half-enclosed, the solarium half-formed, and sprinted across the endless stretch of green yard toward the bushes and trees in the back, seeking the cool of overhanging branches, slapped the trunk of the dogwood, screaming *Safe* and then legs folded and bend on the impossibly rough edges of the blades of grass. Their mother was out of town visiting one of her sisters, hoping to get the sister to call, or maybe even visit, their father who was much changed since he started going to church and stopped drinking, had given them five dollars to go to the Convenient, but Leah wouldn't go, promising to give Jacob her half if he would pretend that they'd gone there and bought candy, so they larked in the yard.

Jacob said he didn't like going to school, because the other children didn't like him and the teacher didn't like him and he didn't like going to church because the Sunday school teacher didn't like him and the stories scared him and he was scared he was going to be bad and the Creature was going to get him like it got Jonah. An ant crawled across his leg, the barest tiny thing, so small Jacob couldn't even feel its six legs on his one leg, and Leah looking down and seeing the ant told Jacob that he didn't have to be afraid, that nothing bad would happen to him at school and nothing bad would happen to him at church and all he had to do was do everything she said and listen to her and then she was up and her young legs were leaping from the shadow to light across the yard, and Jacob jumped up and ran, the ant gone from his leg in a cataclysm too profound for it to comprehend, and Leah was an unstoppable bolt, nearly to the house before Jacob had risen, before his own legs were moving and exploded through the door and through the kitchen and down the hall, Leah disappeared ahead of him, into the house, the rooms and rooms, the shaded windows, the ticking of the old clock in the hall, the small toy car that he loved and never let go of, a small blue Bug, still in his hand, and Jacob called for her as he stood in the hall and listened to the house as it creaked and moaned softly and he began to softly speak Leah's name again when the door to the basement just behind him slowly opened and a hand reached out from the darkness and took hold of his shoulder and pulled him into the void. As he began to scream, another hand covered his mouth and at his ear she said, "Shhh." Leah held him there in the doorframe, at the top of the steps that lead down to the dark basement. They heard something and both fell silent. "Listen."

"Is someone knocking walls?" There was a rhythmic creaking upstairs, and they listened to the sound, faint and soft like a knuckle on wood. It continued unabated for a few minutes and then muffled voices and they scrambled for the doorknob and spilled out of the basement, slamming the door behind them and then they burst forth again from the house out into the bright but waning light of the day and were again racing across the grass, but they did not stop at the line of trees, beating the bushes and flying across a neighbor's yard into another street where they finally stopped to leap and laugh. Later, their father angrily asked them if they'd been in the house that afternoon and Jacob pretended to eat candy.

Pale mountains made of water, the forgotten things, old memories, unexceptional moments they fade before Leah opened her eyes, all off in some unknown place together, a land of reverberations.

A black clock hanging on a white wall above the white sink, had stopped. A yellow field on her grandfather's farm full of cows, heads lowered and lowing to themselves. A long wall, dry masonry, separated the field from his yard. In the center, an oak or maple or elm. Not knowing its name, she cannot remember what it was. The cows are gone, the field is empty, the tree has a disease of the bark. The fire goes out. The night remains night, however.

A replica of the night sky crudely described on the ceiling above their beds by their father. Glow in the dark stars in the shape of Orion and Cassiopeia and Ursa Major and Ursa Minor and Cancer and Taurus. During the day the cracks in the plaster were black rivers cutting a dry and white land, a bare place with no civilization. At night, the universe appeared before them and they watched as it faded and then there was nothing but the dark and the occasional light from a passing car.

The morning was warm. Each drop of light suspended in the air. Against the bricks, the ceiling was a universe of sun-bleached geometric forms and figures waiting for young imaginations to see them. A small head, muzzle drawn to a short point, a mark, a black eye or nostril. Running nymphs. Beasts raising up on hind legs. Maws gaping. Thick fingers. A long neck created by a drizzle of lines. Two bodies filled with scribble, arching outward with uneven appendages toward one another, but an insurmountable gulf of ceiling between them and all of those stars and their fading light.

"I've seen him," Jacob says.

"Shush!"

When they were in the bathroom, washing the small cuts on their hands, their mother stopped in the door, her arms full of clothes. She looked at her children with a soft smile. She'd been angry when they both came home in ruined clothes, wet and reeking, and Jacob crying, and she'd been ready to take a belt to their thighs, but then she'd seen that they'd hurt themselves, the bloody palms, and she'd been filled with guilt at how angry she'd been and how that anger had felt so good in her lungs for a moment. "Wash up, you all. Wash up." *Tomorrow*, she thought, *I'll pray about it.* She was tired of praying about her husband, so it felt good to have something else to worry about. Wash where the blood reeks of splintered soil.

Mrs. Shepherd twisted around and looked back at the man. He flicked his tongue out and wagged it below his brown moustache. He would one day fall from a scaffold and end up in the University of Kentucky Medical Center in Lexington with a tube in his throat that allowed a machine to breathe for him. Unable to move, staring at the ceiling for hours when he woke, before they would prop him up and set the television on a station. This, however, is still a number of years off. Right now, he was laughing at the woman and grabbing himself.

The morning air, low lying, pregnant with morning light. Sunlight smeared over the hills and green leaves of the now full trees. All was still, dappled, right. That otherworldly haze draped over the world outside, something reserved for another life.

"I get up pretty early. I start showing houses as early as I can. My husband teaches. We've lived here for years. I spend a lot of time driving around, but it's not so bad, the countryside and all—"

This commute gave Mrs. Shepherd lots of time in her gold Oldsmobile with her audiobooks. *Six Steps to Personal Success* and *Wealth and Weight Loss*. Each morning, golden sunrise behind her, she masticated maple-flavored sausage biscuits from Hardee's, and each evening, sunset behind her, she sipped Biggie-sized sodas from Wendy's. It kept her out of the house.

"I have a daughter. She runs a nonprofit for women." There is a moment that she faces when meeting with new clients, the questions about her family, whether she says she has two children and then has to explain the loss of one or whether she says that she only has one and lets it go at that. When she has told people that she has two children and they ask what her son does, she is faced with a second choice—how much detail to go into. "We lost him." Or, "He's gone." Or— What was too much? Too much for her, for the person listening. She never knew the right euphemism. Her instincts told her that people did not like being on the receiving end of such a story, especially in a business setting, when sitting down with a young couple, looking to buy their first home. A young couple with children of their own. Usually she opted to only name Leah and explain Leah's work, which most people reacted positively to, but on occasion she met someone whom she felt a harmony with, who she sensed would be receptive to the story. Or perhaps she was only giving in, to the detriment of her sales numbers that month, to the sudden and periodic need to speak it, to give voice to her life, her loss. Perhaps the people she told didn't want to hear this sad story any more than any other person at 10:15 in the morning looking at a 3 br, 2.5 bath, starter home in great neighborhood, great schools, central AC. Maybe her instincts were failing her and she was reading these few wrong. Or maybe some people cared enough that she could sense it. She didn't know. "Look at how the light comes in."

"You think he's really going to do something? Like come here and shoot us up or something?"

"No, that would mean that he had to put pants on and go out."

The abandoned pool of the Old Country Club was empty, an hourglass. The empty hourglass full of broken glass and sun-bleached cans glittering with slugs. On the crumbling plaster was written names of loves long since dead. Night held remaining moon. In the halls, cries were peeling paper. Horses sense haints. "Some of you are living in loneliness. Like a bird in a sack." The preacher shuffled his papers, forgot the passage. In the summer, weeks are all the same. "The soil cries with his blood that only the Lord can hear. This mark to protect him against every hand."

And then her father was gone again, having gone out, back to work. Lost in the spilling arcs, after father, leaves turn white. A storm. He drove her past the cemetery and she could not tell which of them was laughing. *For the Public Health, there shall be no corpses in our water.* On the page, the plain page, mother's face, on the street, mother's face, on the screen, mother's face. Fruit rots. Smells sweet. *Who remembered his name?* Crawlers out of nowhere crawled along the walls. A town drowned. Doors battered frames in idle currents. Drifted along the edge in the foamy water thick with wrack. White froth. Splintered branches. Cast of papers and cans. The whole marina burned. A careless cigarette flicked where someone was fueling. A billow. A ripple on the water. Terrified knowing that something unseen moved beneath her.

One girl ate mud. She howled by those two trees on the far end of the playground. We dug for geodes and washed them in the rain, wished for car wrecks and loneliness, dying in each other's wishes and our own, all the while, rippling like the skirt of bells, trying to ruin one another's prayer. They held hands. In the sinkhole, black water. Papers bloomed a frost of white around it. Just junk that flittered out of truck beds. A victory of garbage, but where did the garbage go, all of this trash, all of this red wrapping paper ripped in spring from already forgotten trash, where did it go? Papers blossom on the slope by bushes.

Through the clatter, the neighborhood boys climbed the tree, higher, past where Leah climbed, where she came down crying over the splinter, past the rusted wire that passed through the trunk, puckered wooden lips holding it in place and that splinter in her palm and she watched. The man laughing with a glowing red light in his mouth raised the BB gun and fired at the boys' bare thighs, already red from the gray bark.

The town, sunk low and spread out, a watery sigh rolled off of the slow breathing heaves of hills to the south, lost momentum in between swells of slow-swooning rock. At night, light pin-holed the shapeless ground and shimmered through the murk of trees and houses, a quiet chunk of fallen above in danger of being swallowed. Low sunk and spread out, frightfully black water seeping through the soles of her shoes, old street names. Fluorescent street lamps did nothing to empty the darkness but deepened it with soft light that showed edges and sounded depths. Summer arrived later than usual, scented with weight, slurring along the ground, refracting sullen rock and earth, the ground doubles, the sighing ground sighed. Cascading hollers, bright plumes. From their father's shoulders Jacob saw the neighbor set off fireworks. Jacob's eyes wide. Jacob's mouth open. The whole night drawn in light. Her mother sat on the step and they watched the joyous fires and all of that color with squealing strings of sound, sparkling spirits chased the neighborhood boys down the driveway and through the yard and the neighbor's father looned. The Shepherds then went in, the lights done. Night like catfish, gills pushed stars to the surface of her face.

"Jacob!" Mrs. Shepherd called. "Jacob! Goddamnit. Jacob!"

THE OFFICE FULL OF WHISPERS, HUMS, AND GLASS. Storage for years of client files. Worn hardwood floors with worn rugs. Outdated copies of the Kentucky Revised Statutes sat on shelves, undisturbed. The women waited with their children and Leah Shepherd met with staff to work on caseload distribution and met with clients to divine what was needed.

The woman told about what happened to her daughter. "The boys were howling and it filled up the school and they didn't do nothing about it." Leah flipped through the file, the pleadings, the invoices, the notices, without looking up.

Below the department store's gleaming fluorescent lights trapped in plastic honeycombs, fathers with children chirped along, the young bleating and bobbing, mothers swayed sweetly as they talk at babies and young husbands with young wives filled up plastic carts with the first supplies for their first homes, first bedsheets and first detergent bottles, impulsively adding a bit of chocolate or a small bag of fruit-flavored candy, and then, handing over weathered bills or signing a credit slip, they slipped out into the evening, the new night, bags in hand, eager to get home and put everything in its place.

———————

Mrs. Shepherd burned a candle on the stove to destroy the dominion of the smell that had crept into the house over the winding years. Yellow-edged books annotated with mildew. A possum waited in the green trash can. Another sip of sherry in secret after a long night. Leah startled herself with her own shadow and in the burrow of her bed, window open, spring again, her mother asking how work was, happy to have her daughter for the night.

The house was alien to Leah, though her parents had lived in it for seventeen years. When she thought about her mother and father rattling around their house, she thought of them in the old house on St. Mildred's Court. When she thought of Main Street, she thought of the department stores and diners and offices that had been there when she was a child, ones that had long since closed, been sold, or changed their names.

There were two Crow Stations, one superimposed atop the other, one seething with light and color and people walking along real sidewalks in the new rays of the young sun and it was not the one she saw out the window of her office, an office that had been hers for several years, but which always looked unreal and borrowed. In the afternoons, as the work day slowed and the women in the office began to get ready to leave for the day, she would sit and look out the window and try and drink any of that old light that might still be out there, recede into the folds of memory that flickered and cut and consumed so many of her hours.

A work-desk. A placid place. Blank gray Formica and illusory wood-grain. Gnats disappearing into a dream, dust on shoes, rainwater evaporating. In a conference room, ceiling tiles droop damply like a jowl. Old plaster buckles and paint peels in bathrooms, but the grant money is gone, given to minimum payments that must be paid on mortgages to keep the bank at bay. The staff sip tangy cups of coffee from chipped mugs and talk about nothing. Leah nods as she gets a cup herself and slips back into her office, ignoring the flashing light on her phone. A door can be closed and the world beyond extinguished. Look at the computer screen, at the numbers in rows, at the **PAGES INTENTIONALLY LEFT BLANK**— And then sips her cup of coffee. Eventually you learn to not see the horrid design of the wallpaper peeling around you.

The nonprofit was incorporated as a 501(c)3 in 1988 by a group of Harrod County business people, church leaders, and Judge Whitehead to provide basic services to low income women and their children in the community. The nonprofit's original director retired in the fall of 2006 and in 2007 Leah Shepherd was announced as executive director. Ms. Shepherd is a Crow Station native. She graduated from Crow Station High School in 1990, Transylvania University in 1994 with a degree in economics and from North Carolina State University with a masters in nonprofit management. Prior to this position, Ms. Shepherd worked for various public interest groups in Lexington and Frankfort. All are very pleased to have Ms. Shepherd—

An old picture of two children, brother and sister, in church clothes standing in front of a fire hydrant, his hair bleached blond and nose sunburned and her arms around his shoulders and her face turned up, mouth open in song, eyes closed, arm out and palm up, cupping pools of sunlight and the boy looking directly at the camera, eyes small and black and wet, mouth set, small and angry.

Mrs. Shepherd couldn't find the picture she was looking for, the one she wanted to frame and give to Leah for her desk. She called out to her husband who was in the garage, but he didn't answer. She kept looking, but never found it and never gave Leah a picture for the desk in her office at her new job.

Wooden rockets on strings.

It had been an oppressively scented summer afternoon—lilac and manure in the air like the white seeds of a dandelion released by pursed lips. The brightly colored pictures of men, women, and children in fine clothes that shone like fires. She made up elaborate stories about each picture for Jacob—fantasias of child princes and glittering wooden attendants, parents dying of grief over the death of a child, a beautiful princess, bare and reclined, broken hearted, throwing herself into the hearth upon the death of her betrothed, her teeth small and smile endless, like a shoreline. Towers of pastel blue and orange light. Monstrous men in black robes, lurking in the shadow of crypts and tombs with bright eyes, singing softly in unknown modes, spiriting off young maidens and the young maidens escaping, bloody but free, fleeing across the edge of hills as night fell toward the very end of the kingdom, which is the end of everything, even Leah uncertain what exists beyond the last line of her story. All in a sunset of colors of which she could not even guess the names.

Jacob begged for more stories but Leah left to go find the neighborhood boys out in the streets and yards with hopes that they would let her play and listen to them curse.

When Leah moved back to Crow Station, she was surprised to find that she didn't know anyone. She expected to see old classmates or people from church that she knew, but it was as though the whole of the town had been replaced. "Everyone you know probably moved away or died," her mother said one evening when they met for dinner at the new restaurant built on the bypass. Her mother shrugged. Her father was looking for the waitress for a refill. Leah was relieved.

"I still have two brain damages they can't fix." Leah wrote and the woman smiled.

Leah was a listener. She would not say a *good listener* because that implied a level of active compassion that Leah felt she lacked, despite her job and despite her best efforts and despite all of the people who tearfully hugged her and thanked her and all of the people who wrote her letters, even years later, telling her how her help got them back on their feet, despite all of the people she knew who remarked upon her *obvious compassion* and *tireless caring*, despite all of this, she didn't feel it. It didn't come naturally. Her immediate reaction was something akin to terse irritation. The women wire thin or spilling out of too-tight clothing with rough-mouthed children or children quiet to the point of concern. Drugs, alcohol, men, their curses were the same but impossibly varied in their separate shades. Leah knew what everyone was going to say and listened with concealed impatience. And yet each time was surprised by some unexpected thorn, some quiver of fact that suddenly made the alien face before her real, and Leah crumbled before it, reaching out her hand and promising help. The twinge of pain in her eyes was misinterpreted by the women as gentle sympathy, and they felt relief that they'd been heard. One who left college to care for a mentally handicapped sibling. One who was left by a seemingly good man in the night. One who'd fought against disease. One who'd taken in these children that weren't hers and just needed to get to her next paycheck so that all could eat.

She was able to keep these feelings in and to present nothing but the most generous smile and gentle touches on an arm or a shoulder and those non-committal grunts that signal to a speaker that *she is listening*, but she felt it and it bothered her that she felt that way.

"They's just screaming and screaming but I ain't never heard them."

But she was good at listening. She listened to the women talk all day. She listened to their children. She listened to the staff talking idly at their desks to spouses on their cell phones or to catty chatter in the kitchen break room. She listened to people at tables next to her at restaurants and to attorneys talking to clients in the hallways at the courthouse and to children arguing in grocery stores and to old people talking to whoever will pause long enough to listen. Leah listened, whether she wanted to or not, and she wondered what it would have been like to be someone else.

"They traded breath all morning and then ate lunch in front of the television."

She listened and she watched, everyone bleeding everyone else's stories, even the ones they promised not to tell, all too good to keep to themselves.

"No one can hear us. Come on."

At the school, ghosts spoke from the pipes in the winter.

Prior to the lawsuit, Leah Shepherd had nearly saved up enough for a down payment on a small ranch house, built circa 1968, in a small subdivision just outside of town called Streamland. She'd been renting a house within walking distance of work for years and saving what she could, but the suit took her savings and her retirement and she ended up moving not into a house of her own but into the one-bedroom apartment on the bypass, and at night with the window open, she listened to the trees and at dusk she walked in the woods and wondered about the woman she saw slumping around town. That filthy woman. Her long hair in greased tangles. Her face set in a sullen scowl. Her back bent beneath her backpack. Where was she right then? In a dimly lit room with walls ruined by rain, plaster buckling with veins of black mold. Behind a dumpster unsuccessfully holding out her hand for help getting up off the ground. Some place with the smell of damp. Some place with the smell of ripe bodies. Why not in a field in fresh air? Why not by a stream in fading light? Why not still in a small room? The woods drew in dark around Leah lost in thought.

Standing on the corner, before the judicial center, Leah Shepherd watched a tall man with salt-and-pepper hair bubble at the sight of a cigarette butt on the ground, between bricks. The exhausted nub contained a few happy puffs still. He bent to retrieve it, swinging long arms and rained joy. With the courthouse bell, it is time for work, so all went to work or to wait for the bailiff to unlock the doors so that they may go on in.

"Oh, honey, listen, just so morbidly obese...I don't know why I looked it up on the Internet while at the house alone... but yeah, he died...but I can't bring myself to make up his bed...I had the child with me yesterday...She wanted to see his father...I said to him, I said, What is your problem...yes it is my perception...a game, a whole big game...I am sick of being played for a fool…looking at women…smile…checking your house out…yeah, yeah, yeah."

Some mornings, the sheriff's deputies paraded prisoners to the courthouse for preliminary hearings tethered to one another. The deputies, four or five, in tan and brown, short cropped hair, shoulder CBs joshed and hummed, talked and joked. A cluster of coughing guffaws fluttering up. They called out to each other and their eyes wrinkled. The prisoners in orange jumpsuits, together waist-to-waist. Wrists bound penitently at the hip, fingers fingering fingers. They didn't jaw. What would be worth saying? It all is what it is. So they sauntered, heads lolling on necks. They were a stream wishing for a single smoke in the morning air. Young men in no rush to get on with anything. The bell in the courthouse tower clanged the hour and they slipped inside the heavy glass door. Families stood by and watched. They rang with sorrows, their clapper tongues clapped lip, mouth, sounding waist, shoulder, head, and crown. They tolled: bring cousins, sisters, neighbors. Cell phones bubbled with incoming messages. Thumbs texted truncated tales to someone, somewhere. Outside on cement steps, they smoked, pitching butts to bricks, left to smolder.

"I am not a vindictive person, but I want him to be in pain. God help me. I'm a Christian, but I want him to suffer."

"The interest rate is just too high."

"I'm daydreaming."

There was a fountain outside the courthouse. AGUA ESTA MALA FAVOR DE NO BEBER. A group of men in jean shorts and Polos set up a small amplifier and began to preach the Word. They sang hymns. The air conditioners in the bank building across the street dripped water on the heads of those skulking by, trying not to be noticed. Purple stretch pants, high-waisted, acid-washed, wrinkled, rumpled, untucked t-shirts, Sunday best, suits crisp and new, sport coat, tie tacks, pressed, tucked, contacts instead of glasses, tattoos revealed when coughs, wheezes, crutches, motorized wheelchairs. Poor surgery, poor thing, poor surgery. Young bailiffs lounged by the metal detector like young bathers at a pond in the spring, wands in lap. "So it was me and Chris and Hanglade."

"Hanglade? What's he doing?"

"Hanglade? Going to school."

The sky was bunched and soiled batting, the contours of which are lit by some sun that cannot be seen.

"Would you send her a card? She's really depressed. She feels alone. Just get a little one from the Dollar Store. Just a fifty cent one. She never gets to see her son. Just say a little something. For her…" The copy machine overwhelmed the rest.

The spine read: *Dead Bodies* through *Declaratory Judgments*. It rained and leaves gullied past. The telephone rang. Dead bodies broken waiting for names called broken waiting. Blood giving new life. The telephone rang and rang and rang. On a post, in the spring, two birds, one on another. The small tree with bark like peeling wallpaper sat alone and considered the snack cake wrapper at its feet, half-hidden in the dead leaves. The parking lot was empty except for a black Escalade half-hidden in back of the office of a lawyer who lost his license. Perhaps it waits for nightfall, which came soon enough. In the evening, a last light overwhelmed by flashing blue and red licking sidewalk and brick. A car stopped on the side of the street. Whir in front of a yellow-green hedge. Off-white Mercury Cougar full of stuffed animals. Purple bears pressed into taupe puppies and sun-bleached humanoids spilled on the backseat and dashboard. Nameless forms with splitting seams. When she was a young girl, Leah carried a stuffed rabbit with her to the summer camp and on the last day gave it to the deaf boy that had played with her all week. He had a large head, large eyes, glasses, and others yelled mean things at them while she made the rabbit dance for the boy. She gave it to him not because she liked him enough to give away her most precious possession, but because giving her rabbit away hurt not to have it. At home in her room, she would think of that rabbit and begin to cry and her mother would come in and hold her, feeling Leah's warm tears and they would be quiet. In the dark, in her mother's embrace, she would sink inside herself, past her own pitiful little sorrow, her room and the night and her mother and the rabbit glimmering smaller and smaller on the distant surface of his being, and then it was morning and her mother was gone and there were birds trilling in the branches outside of her window. The rabbit had been Jacob's before and she'd always been jealous of it.

All is wonder as the bricks of the old train station are swallowed by the creeping feet of ivy and moss. All is wonder as the left turn signals of the three cars in front of her pass in and out of sync slowly, phasing through all possible combinations in sequence. It is night, she crept toward home and the courthouse bell sang some closing hymn.

"Leah! Leeaaaah!"

She woke in the void, forgetting where she was for a moment, and remembered the faint light from the hallway, Jacob sitting on the corner of his bed, saying, "Can you hear it? Can you hear it howling?" and there it was, the howling howling howling and they shivered in their beds and listened to the rutting and snuffling just outside of their room and she whispered something to Jacob, some apology lost in the howling and they could smell their missing blood.

In the morning, Leah, tired even with an extra cup of coffee, listened to a woman talking on her cell phone to her daughter in the break room. "Bless," the woman said, implying judgment. Leah sipped her coffee, flipped through the local news section of the paper and listened to two other women talk about children vomiting. How far into the woods does the path by the stream go, Leah wondered as she burned her lips and walked to her office. What if she just kept walking?

"So, I guess I'll never feed him that again, but it was just weird, but my mother said—"

When Leah first brought communion, the woman smiled and Leah read the prayer and the woman chewed the small wafer and sipped slowly the small plastic cup of grape juice. They talked for an hour, a talk that was mostly silence, but which was warm and left Leah feeling happy. The next time Leah brought communion, a month later, the woman smiled, but did not remember Leah. Leah repeated her name, louder, but the woman shrugged and smiled. They went through the same actions as before, the prayer, the body, the blood, the sitting and talking, the pause, and Leah, disappointed that the woman did not remember her, said she would be back in a few days.

Leah began visiting the old woman once or twice a week, spending an hour or two just sitting. Sometimes she brought groceries or small gifts. The woman began to remember Leah, or said she did. Sometimes the woman called Leah by other names, the woman's daughters or granddaughters, perhaps. Leah didn't know. There were pictures of children and grandchildren scattered through the house, a nice house, but Leah tried not to look at them.

And Leah would bring communion and she would bring groceries which she bought with her own money and they would sit and one day the woman said she wanted to do something nice for Leah, but Leah demurred. The old woman insisted. "You've done so much," she said and Leah said, "No, no, no," but the woman wrote a check to Leah. At first, Leah wasn't even going to cash it, but then she didn't want to insult the woman, who asked several times if Leah had cashed the check, so Leah cashed it, but used the money to buy something nice for the woman. Then the woman asked Leah to run some errands for her and Leah did, because Leah said she would do anything for the old woman, who must have been in her mid-eighties, and so the woman gave her a list of things she needed and Leah got them for her and the woman gave Leah her ATM card and asked Leah to go to the bank for her and Leah did. Leah did what she was asked. The woman offered Leah money and Leah took it because the woman wanted Leah to take it and she reimbursed herself for the purchases because that is what the woman would have wanted and when the woman said she wanted to leave Leah something, Leah contacted an attorney, but only because the woman wanted her to do so. Leah did what the woman wanted. And when the woman insisted on making the little figurines in the basement for the children in the church, little figures with little felt clothes that the woman made with her knobby, trembling hands in the poor light of the basement, Leah asked her not to because it was too hard for her to get up and down, but the woman never listened.

One of the houses on the road that Leah drove each morning to work had a small dogwood tree out front. From the branches of the tree hung blue glass bottles. They were tied with graying string and spun slightly in the breeze. An elderly woman sitting outside with a black dog by her side. She had a green kerchief on her head and she waved at the cars as they passed. One day, she was gone but the bottles remained.

One evening, the sky was purple and the clouds were orange. They took on strange shapes. Dead grass grew. Paved lots were full of cracks with yellow stems pushing through. There was a taste to the water—dense and green. That woman walking along a country road, her boots along the gravel shoulder. In a pair of pants that were once nice, but were now soiled in the seat and the knees. A nice pair of pants that she must have been given by the Salvation Army. What was in the backpack that she carried on her bent back? Leah passed and tried to look into her rearview mirror to see the woman's face, but there was a bend in the road and all Leah could see were trees dressed in the purple shadows of early evening.

A dead dog was found in the road that no one recognized. Everyone at the office was talking about it. There was one shoe on the side of the road. There were strange messages in the personals. The telephone rang, but there was no one there. The telephone rang and there was just clicking. The television flickered and clouds rolled in from the wrong direction. Grandchildren called their grandmothers without having to be told. A strange man helped a woman who'd dropped her things. He did not give his name. A young woman living alone moved back home and claimed the baby had no daddy.

In the waiting area someone laughs and spills sweet tea on the monthly financial reports. Her granddaughter has called and is getting married.

Clients, in their best clothes and with children, smile politely and chomp Starlight mints. Joy is no cause for the cessation of work.

The boy wouldn't hold still. His mother begged him, "Jesse, Jesse, honey, please hold still, I need to talk to this woman, please, Jesse."

Leah turned to the boy, smiling, and asked him, "Would you like a book to read? We have some books." The boy shook his head and wriggled. His mother said, "You like to read don't you? Jesse?" The boy stopped moving and looked at Leah. She asked, "Where do you go to school?" He looked at his mother and she said, "Tell the nice lady where you go." The boy didn't say anything. He was slumped down in the chair so far that his back and head were on the seat. The woman sighed and said, "He goes to Toliver." Edna L. Toliver Elementary School was Crow Station's oldest school. "That's where I went to school when I was your age," Leah said to the boy, leaning toward him, smiling. He was a cute boy, she thought. A round head and plump face and quick grin. "Do you want the woman to get you a book to read?" his mother asked again and the boy said, "No, I don't want to read." Leah gave him an exaggerated look of mock shock and said, "You don't like to read? But reading is so much fun and Toliver has such a great library full of cool books about mythology and detectives and castles." The boy stopped moving and said, "I don't like it." His mother took his arm gently and said, "Honey, please, the nice woman—" and Leah said, "Why don't you like it?" She remembered the orange carpet and the high windows that ran along most of the front wall that looked out on the town. "I don't like it because there's a ghost up there." Leah looked at him and didn't say anything and the woman said, "Jesse, honey, what did I tell you about that. Jesse, honey, please," and Leah asked, "A ghost?" and the boy said, "There's a ghost of a boy and everyone said they seen him. I haven't but I am scared to. This one girl said that when she goes up there he looks at her from the hallway and another girl said he tried to touch her hand." The woman said, "Jesse, that's it, how many times do I have to tell you—"

Fragments of light cast across the cosmos reached the blue hood of her blue car. When she was in high school, she rode with her parents to the cemetery to see the stone. The stone signaled that they'd given up, finally.

One night, she snuck into the cemetery with a friend and as they walked, they passed the stone and Leah said, "That grave is empty."

The night cracked. Beyond the trees, a train groaned, its mouth open, slithering between the bent branches.

Leah Shepherd stayed late looking at things on the Internet she shouldn't. She couldn't afford the Internet at her apartment, so she would stay late at work sometimes and if she found something she liked, she would carefully make sure that no one was in the building, no matter how late it was and she took care of herself.

And the boy sunk to the bottom of the sea and the slow churn of the ancient ocean turned his bones to dust and turned the dust to stone and over the silent turning of the bottom of the ocean, no light fell and his name was lost among the shards of bone and shell.

The neighborhood boys were sitting on the curb in the bend in the street, setting off Black Cats and throwing rocks at one another. They wrestled on the pavement, howling and laughing, scraping and bruising each other, skin peeling in leaves of pale pink and lakes of red. Blistered fingers and bruises welling. "Fat fuck." "Fat fuck face. Fag." Picking teeth, the boys howling.

"Hey," Leah said, sidling up, "I heard your yard was haunted."

The neighborhood boys craned their lumpy necks at her and lolled their red eyes. Their faces erupted. "Listen, listen, listen." This little girl drove them crazy. What was she? Like ten or something. And that little baby brother, always crying. But this they listened to because they were very bored. They'd broken already that summer everything that they could get their hands on. And so, summer being what it was, they listened.

"How do you know?"

"I can't tell you. This girl said."

"Girl? I thought you liked boys."

"Fag."

"Fag's for a guy that sucks dicks. She's not a fag. She's a lezzie."

"Listen," undisturbed and eager, unsure what they meant, but not wanting to betray ignorance, she insisted and they began to sway and circle. So they listened. The boys. Howling and howling. And crackling cracks in the curbs. "That there was a girl who lived in your house and she died because this guy she loved died in the war and she killed herself and her parents buried her in the side-yard and put that pond in." A hole and a hole and a hole. "No, listen, listen, it really happened. The girl told me it was the truth and then swore on her mother's grave and showed me a bone." They bellowed cackles at holes.

"Okay, so what? Okay, so show us."

And Leah led the boys in the gate of the walled garden where it was quiet. A slight breeze slithered. Though summer, bare legs and arms goose-fleshed. Impatient, the boys akimbo and *contrapposto*. Lulled by the silence there in the garden behind the wall. In that moment, the possibility of a secret seemed real. They listened to her. Flemish bond, ten feet high, discolored by lichens and moss. Brick paths around the green pool of water. In the corners, planters with dry and dying plants. Brown leaves. Fallen petals. Broken stalks. And the pool's glaucous eye, lidless, idle. What odd portents had it been quietly privy to? The bending branches of old oak and elm trees outside the garden bent curiously over the walls, cut the sunlight into suggestion of light and with dry voice, spoke.

"Her body," Leah said and the boys listened and the world listened. "Her body was buried here. This is where her father, heartbroken, buried her remains. I didn't tell you, but she shot herself, taking her father's gun from his desk while he was at work. She held it up to her eye and pulled the trigger. There was nothing left of her face. Her eyes and brains and nose were everywhere. Her father came home and found her and wept for his daughter. He felt so guilty, like he'd pulled the trigger. He carried her down here to the yard and buried her and built this around her." A loose brick moved at her touch and the boys crowded around. Clouds of starlings passed by above. The boys pulled up the brick. With their fingertips, prying.

The sound of the metal gate behind them slamming the brick wall sent shudders through them and high squeals and standing there was Jacob in his powder-blue overalls just like a baby would wear. "I told you to stay home," she said.

"You said we'd play." The boys began to laugh. Something escaped from the garden. One boy noticed a nest in a pear tree, reached up in the sudden crowing of changing voices and tossed it down, dashing a blue egg to the interlocked bricks. Blue against yellow-green moss and lichen. She screamed at Jacob and he keened and the boys began to wander away, tongues aflame with glee. The little baby in his saddle oxfords. She began to follow but Jacob reached for her arm and she pushed him down, only registering for a moment the tide of pleasure that this brought and he fell rear first into the slosh and muck of the reflecting pool. Rotten water. The boys erupted and Jacob was silent, still, staring at Leah. "How could you do that to your own brother," they said. "You're a fucking bitch." They began to cackle. They touched their own crotches and called her a slut and were gone.

"Please don't tell mother what I did. I'm so sorry. Please don't tell." Jacob said nothing. He walked home wet and cold.

The next day, their mother sang. "Rise and shine and give God the glory." Leah and Jacob rose and wandered downstairs, wobbling on still sleeping legs like the risen dead, hungry. They ate. Crispy bacon and blackened biscuits. They drank milk from colorful plastic cups. They'd all forgotten the spanking for the ruined clothes, still wet with reflecting pool water. "Get dressed for church. Come on now."

Clothes out for them the night before. A dress with a square collar and small slacks and a clip-on tie. They wriggled in like worms wriggling into a corpse.

"I don't want to go," Jacob said. "Please." He pouted and stormed down the steps and out the front door. She just sat downstairs in the chair in the living room, watching him pout down the front walk through the window, like he did every Sunday, happy to see him gone.

"Okay, let's go. Where's your brother?" She pointed at the door. Her mother opened it and began yelling for her son. "Jacob! Goddamn." She looked at her watch. "Goddamn." Her father came down the steps, pulling tie tight, and looked at the women of his house and said Mrs. Shepherd had to teach Sunday school and serve communion and could not be late. She asked her husband to find where Jacob was hiding and meet them at church and, prodding Leah along, left. Leah kept expecting to see him sitting by his favorite tree, on the curb with his round face in his hands, but they didn't see him and Mrs. Shepherd continued to curse to herself. Leah almost said something to her mother, told her something, but didn't. They walked on.

In her Sunday school class, Leah learned about the Tower of Babel. The children sat around the room in hard wood chairs and listened to the Sunday school teacher talk, and Leah slipped into a reverie raveled out and it was only when everyone began to get up and walk out that she returned to the room, looked around confused. She looked into the room where the younger children sat with the pictures of Joseph they colored, his bright coat in waxy rainbow scribble, but he wasn't in there. In the sanctuary, she sat next to her mother who kept looking around for Mr. Shepherd, but he didn't come. The service started and they sang hymns and listened to verses and her mother got up and walked to the front to take the trays of bread and grape juice and circulate them through the congregation and then she returned to her seat and the minister gave a short sermon on something, but Leah had faded away again, thinking of something else, her eyes open but seeing only what her mind fluttered in front of her and then the organ droned and everyone stood and walked out after the minister, and Leah and her mother walked home and Mr. Shepherd was standing outside and as they walked up he said, "Don't worry—"

That night, they waited for someone to call. "Hello?" And then a pause. Her father's face and her mother's face and a fly between the blinds and the window pane. It rasped and flounced. She turned the rod and the blinds closed and its soft battering was lost in the sound of her mother.

When she was grown, Leah could not remember what happened next. She sometimes thought that maybe she finished changing out of her church clothes and went into her bedroom or she went into the kitchen and found her mother sitting there or she came into her room, looking down at her in her underwear and began to say something—maybe that happened later. There'd been policemen in the house all evening and men in coats and ties. The telephone rang and rang. She didn't remember hearing her mother cry, but she could see her mother crying. And the telephone again and again. At some point, her father was home and put her to bed—where had he been? Walking. Looking. All night long. It was Sunday and her brother had not wanted to go to church. When her father found her, she was asleep in the yard.

Sometimes as she listened to the women at her work she could feel herself fill with an incredible feeling of disgust and irritation. The children wallowed on the floor or they threw the donated toys and the mothers sat mum or bellowed at the small things and just as the feeling rose, a sudden black point of pity and affection rose up inside, along with a sliver of shame. And then she smiled, looking the women in the eye, held out her hands, held out her arms, hugged them, told them she would see what she could do. Where they could be placed. Where might be able to help with a job and the women smiled at her and thanked her and the children wallowed and quaked with young voices, but that is what children do. The waiting room walls adorned with the crayon confusion of children's drawings. The telephone on her desk rang, but she could not get to it in time.

At first they didn't say anything, but when it was dark and her father put her in the bed, under the sheets that needed a change, she able to feel the grit on her feet, she asked him where her brother was. "We don't know." And then, "Don't worry." That was the last they talked about it.

Leah fell asleep outside the night after her brother disappeared, outside to get away from the sounds inside, and she saw two little girls in brilliant calico dresses walk from the garage and climb up the maple tree. They didn't come down, not that she saw. The night was silent. The stars were silent. The grass was silent. The world was empty.

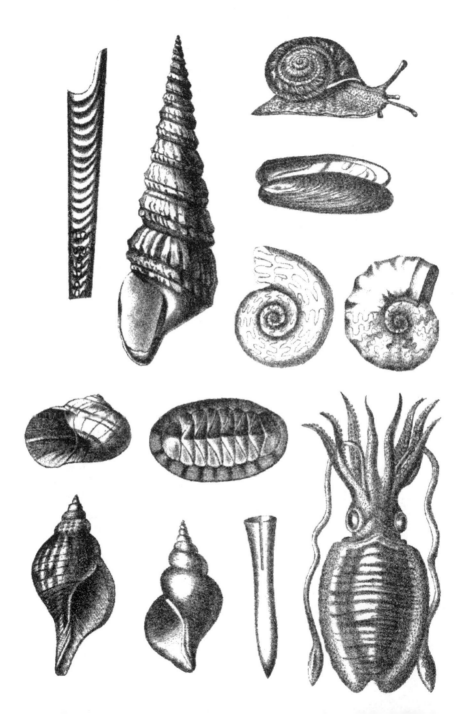

CROW STATION, KENTUCKY: A GIRL AT THE window watching a shift in the shadows, listening to the sound of the night, the glittering dark above her bed, her father's hands having placed the sky there, cracked plaster rivers among constellations of dead boys and girls, but by morning the vault of the heavens is nothing but the white ceiling, though the corners do flutter with dusty webs her parents have not noticed and her brother's bed. A boy crouched in his room, praying to the sound of voices rising from the register softly wishing that the creature with the long claws would come and take them all away. A teacher waiting in the parking lot of the school for his student, the smell of her body still on his sweater, a duffle bag to hide the surprise, the parking lot wet from recent rain, the blacktop's contours filled with miniature lakes, the spreading rainbow of oil on the face of the water, the teacher's hands damp, the smell still rising to his nose, but he's cried all he can and all that is left is the Lord's Work. An empty blue car on the side of the road. The party, the men with drinks, sloshing and spilling, calling names, the smell of burning somewhere, names holler listen rolling across the ground all the girls they think falling into themselves who wouldn't want this falling into themselves. The department store, closed, the windows reflecting the passing people, the display racks standing still but empty, though somewhere in the endless dark of now unused inner offices, boxes of receipts, decades of transactions, await another life. A man waiting in his office resisting the urge to call the hospital for the seventh time in an hour to check on her condition, when the sound of steps comes down the hall and he sets the receiver on its rest and pretends to work. A bonfire on a distant hill, orange light in the black night, hanging insubstantial in the void. A bonfire in a distant field, the gleaming grills of pickup trucks in a semi-circle, windows open so all could hear the sick system. Garth Brooks and Jodeci. En Vogue and Anthrax. Judas Priest and Onyx. Snow and Alan Jackson. A bonfire dying down to a charred blot in the starless night, pale bodies passed out in the beds of the pickup trucks, young men and young women, and in the total blank, a voice. The woman's shaved head in the sun, feeling the sun, the warm rays, heavy rain as the boat bobbed, she removed her hat and her husband smiled at her and removing their life vests, they dove into the cool brown water of the man-made lake and swam around to the far side of the boat, in the shade of the bending trees in the inlet and found one another. A woman walking in the woods, listening for crying that she thought she heard. The muddy shore, brown and green, the brown water cooling in the shade. The buzz and whir of the trees. The clicking trees, the clacking trees. The silence of crumbling branches and leaves. The jawing of the woods, without beginning and without end and someone walking. A bend in the street and the sun-baked sidewalk with confetti of shadow, a leopard, and just at the bend a person walking away, disappearing around the curve, behind a tree and the street is empty. A secret post office box, a secret credit card, an evening hoping the cell phone does not ring. An evening worrying that the payment on the television set might not make it in time. That the payment on the SUV might not make it in time. A car driving past the house for the fourth time in an hour. A woman killing a colony of ants with a pot of boiling water and all the years' leaves in dunes in the corner of the porch. The sun playing on the surface of the broken glass of the smashed bottle of beer thrown onto the patio in retaliation for a remark about a sister. The sun speaking along the edge of the glass and along the edge of the lite beer. Swill gilded with evening rays. The backyard garden, up mossy steps, in a stroke of sunlight, a distant parental voice, directionless, powerless to the draw of this moment, the distant dogs with the bloody stumps of their excised tails wailing to the distant turn of the neighborhood. A latex werewolf mask, a tent, the night and a knife, the brothers having fought, run and yelled, hollered and beaten walls, crying over insignificance, and one darting in the pale light of the security lamp in the backyard while the other whispered to his friends. The feeling of dirt and dust against dry skin and the rubbing of raw wood against the flesh of calves after having seen them on one another, calling out names and foulness, the pages of the illustrated Bible torn and wet, the tongue of summer heavy on everything. A drive home. A kiss. Divining a body in the dark. Fingers unhooking. Prodding terse and enveloping. Listening under a streetlight. On a swing set in the dark behind the church. Watching the outline of black trees as the warm breath of summer slips down thighs. A pasture cut by a stream, and on the other side, the green rise of a mound, a burial place perhaps and beyond even that, a marsh, webbed with water, fallen logs for lolling arms and the two outstretched, looking up through green light into the dark canopy of black leaves. Two shapes moving through the yard at night. Two shapes in the shade behind the empty department store. Two bodies roving one another. A howl loose and ranging. A howl lifted to the heavens. A howl harrowing the cul de sacs and courts. A window, half open, the voice singing the passing cars' songs. Something left on the doorstep. A bed with sheet thrown back. The gutter on a street. The glass in the gutter on a street. The blades of grass rising through the garbage in the gutter on a street. Aglitter with God's own last light. A voice saying, "She's not doing well." A voice saying, "Were you going?" Blood running into an eye and children swarming the basketball court screaming for the ball. Hook shots awry. The ivy-laced fence around the cemetery. The family no longer gathered, the woman alone straightening the silk flowers she left, looking at her name on the other half of the marker. The realtor walking through the empty house, noting to the young couple that there is no legal requirement to disclose if the previous occupant died of AIDS or if the house is haunted, and though she prepared the real estate purchase contract, the couple were unwilling to sign and she went home angry, though she could not show it to the young couple, and sat in her living room, checking the message on her cell phone and calmed herself by thinking about her mission trip to Africa. A hill and the two sitting, turning to leaves as the breeze speaks their names. A young man's car in pieces across the highway and the state trooper dreading the call to the fiancée. A passing train, never ending. A man who brings his boys to watch it rattle along, listening to old soul songs as the boys pick things up off the ground. A boy talking to a girl, her hands signing, his eyes wishing he could read. The young man's jeans riding low over bony hips, reaching across to where the older man sat, face flushed and a passing train rattled the windows. A dentist dragging a millstone through the town, window rolled down, pointing his finger at God like a pistol, laughing too hard to speak the warning to the world in his heart. A minister walking into a field. A father farting for his son's amusement. The three girls waiting by the window, hoping their father does not come home. Sprawled in a bathtub, gray water cooling, too disinterested to even touch himself, a man remembers with wonder the first time he rubbed himself raw on the bathroom floor of his grandmother's house while she cooked meatloaf and green beans and smoked unfiltered cigarettes, the kitchen windows open to let an autumn breeze in. Weeds growing up high. Grass growing faster than the property manager can handle and the tenant with the dog is standing on the balcony again screaming at the children below and the dog bays and howls and the children laugh and continue to throw gravel, though the rocks arc shy of their target. A glass case with trusses and braces. Metal rods to straighten the back. Bedpans and bottles with tubing. Walls of bottles. Elixirs, tinctures, pills, tablets, philters. A rack with sun-bleached comics. The Gods all dead. A gash across Hercules' eye. Pages grow more brittle each year. A curving counter with a jar for beef sticks and loafing men spilled over the edge, gazing into the surface of their coffee or into the amber remnants of their syrup. Spitting griddle. Chili dogs, chuck wagons, brown burgers spitting on metal plate. A dusty window lets in gray light. Horehound candy, Beech-Nut gum. A long cluttered counter of tin cars in faded boxes waiting for children that have long since grown. Sisters hide here and wait until it is time to go home. A cash register rings and worn bicentennial quarters pass over palms. A boy gone missing. A mother yelling down an empty street. A child hidden in a clothing rack, aware of the switching to come, but unable to help herself. Children range through the department store and caw for candy. A hand in a room in a column of light. At the end of a conveyor in the far back corner of a toy warehouse, young men waiting for the day to start, the electronic tone that tells them to pile the dream houses on the dusty belt. A man offering a book and a look at others of worth, wiping his mouth with the back of his hand, adjusting his glasses, rubbing the back of his neck, peering down at the young face, smiling and feeling in his pockets. Calcium carbonate, limestone, marble, all of the shells of all of the living things crawling along. A sister that is unwell, shriveling in her room as the family prays, as the preacher calls on the family, bends by her bedside, says words as best he can, as the father wakes, washes himself, works all day, and drives home, seeing her blinds closed, knowing the light makes her feel worse, he goes in to see his little girl, praying, smelling the dinner ready downstairs and sits on the side of her bed and listens to the noise of the bypass. A father who wanted silence so much that he went so far as to plan on puncturing his ear drums with knitting needles, but not until after he consulted with a physician under the pretense of researching a novel in which a father wanted silence so bad that he punctures his eardrums with coat hangers. A child choking in her crib while a young parent dozes. Two students in a dark hall, whispering. A girl and her brother, listening in the dark for the sound of a monster moving through their house. On the curb, the broken body of a girl hit by a car as the neighborhood children pool silently. A dog on the bottom of the doctor's in-ground pool. A mother and father silent in the dark bedroom, counting the cars passing, watching their high beams skitter across the walls just like their children used to do, the children that felt like they were still right there, right upstairs asleep in their beds, bunk beds, empty for decades. The principal who still lived at home with his elderly parents, allowing them to cook and clean for him, his wife having left him some years before for reasons that his parents were never entirely clear on, though they were certain that she was a tramp. The woman washing her grown son's clothes. The principal who called the staff in to watch the videotape of the students that he kept in his desk and making lewd comments while some averted their eyes, some walked out, some watched, certain that what they were doing was wrong, but unable to resist and it wasn't until he was called by the paper that he began to regret some of what he'd done. The wooden bones of a whale floating above the children. The woman reading letters left for her, unsigned. A man on the couch, hiding his erection from his wife. The smell of wet and warmth. A car repossessed in the night. Second Notice. Final Notice. Creditors calling places of work. The elderly man who cannot hear, mowing silently in the morning. The children watching the house burn from the back of the truck. Son and daughters who will never marry. Houses rented for lifetimes. Aunts taking young nephews out for dinner at the chicken place and then letting them buy a plastic toy from the dollar store. A trip to the mall with her grandmother, eyes lazing over racks of clothing, mind wandering, the old woman asking, "Do you like it? Do you? Honey?" Dead birds, dying light, cracked pavement, peeling paint, neon lights flickering, pulses of red blue green, traffic piling up, a woman crossing the street, slumping along, dirty clothes, wet clothes, listening to the men as she passes, back bending under backpack, arm swinging, the men stopping to watch her, eyes intent as though she cannot see them, and then they break into a cluck, loudly laughing and looking again, eyes squinting in joy, jaws swaying, cracked pavement, the stream through town, the overpass, the train tracks, the break in the wire fence where she wriggles through and remembers words that were buzzing her, clutter clouds, she darts through into darkening trees, following the curve of the stream. A child screaming during the service, much to his father's disgust. A dog without an eye, under the covers, licking her hand while she sleeps. A dog swimming gaily in the grass. An arm shorter than expected. A cat watching the dark for something to move. The puddle of cat on the floor, somehow always in the narrowing parallelogram of light. A piano clang. Everything gone, everything hidden, the children innocent eyed as their father screams. In bed during the daylight. An animal's head. Black eyes. Black globes. The entire universe in a swirl of glass black and glinting. Women in jeans and in denim skirts, heads covered, hair long and crimped, hair short around sutures. Women with children that sit silent and stare. Women with children that will not sit still. That will not be quiet. That will not shut up. That are bound for a switching if they don't behave. If they don't get right. If they don't listen. Hear me? Children that tear the pages out of books, put the tires of plastic cars in their mouths, shit themselves long after they should have stopped. Children that blood coils swelling air choked with graves. A stucco house on a hill, bent trees bending in, dark rooms, cloudy spring afternoons, a box of puppies and a dentist cutting their tails off while in the back garden his boy begs a neighbor to take off his clothes. A woman reading stanzas by a window, not noticing the fading day, the fading words, fallen asleep. A woman finding a birthmark in the shape of a crab on her date's neck, underneath the heaps of permed hair. The man telling his granddaughter about the tunnels under his house where the slaves used to hide. A man cursing his deaf wife and the blacks that have ruined his name. The doctor reaching into the closet to find the baggy he stashed. The girl in the octagonal room reading Anne Shirley to life. A boy asleep in a cold basement, listening to the steps upstairs though he is alone. The dog watching the man moving naked through the dark house. The sound of thunder across the pasture. The bed unslept in. A world, another whole world, other earths, other stars, the father telling the children, there are other places worse than this, other places better, the sighing sun reaching out its last arms across the ocean of sky and drawing us home. The boy on the jungle gym telling everyone that his cousin let him suck her titties and that she touched his thing. It was the best wedding he'd ever been to. Across a yellow field, a man in thick glasses slipping into the woods with a boy while bells peal. A young man sitting on the blue bridge, pitching his empties down into the water, trying not to care that the girl with his baby is waiting for him to call. The boy parading down the street alone. The sight of sun. The wind moving through trees, branches, low arms, sing song, singing, listen, a voice, listen, the wind speaking through the trees. The bottom of the sea, risen, populated by worn bones and shells. Painted boys whooping. A saxophone rented upon retirement. A mother calling her children's names at an empty window in an assisted living facility and the visitors passing by pretending not to hear. A town in the center of a pasture, a stream and a lake, old houses with peeling paper, old houses with names rattling plaster, wet streets, wild grass and wild flowers erupt from brick and cement, metal rusted red, archipelagos of sound, children in yards and streets scattered about, teens darting from shadow to shadow, singing in voices of light, young men and women driving to work, holding hot drinks between pressed slack thighs, work days trundling, sighing sounds as clicking clocks call to distant hours, retirement parties scheduled for Wednesday mornings, cooling coffee with milky rings, smiles, talk, back to work, the cleaned-out desk, the drive home, a moment to try and remember what happened, the restful moment on a back porch and children calling to say they will be late, they will have to come another time, they are sorry they forgot, the wild grass growing up between stones, in cracks in the pavement, the ivy crumbling mortar, the bricks now loose, the steps a hazard, a warning in passing, the house quiet alone, the television reception for shit, the telephone uncharged for days, the wild grass and wild flowers between the wallpaper pieces, the walls in blooms of green and red and blue and gold, the walls damp and falling, the ceiling buckling, the ivy around the bed, the sky a band of impossible colors, the sound of someone calling out, downstairs, a memory, remember, all of this and the ceiling and the walls nothing but the soft rise and fall of the hills, listen, and they listen and the speaking across the pastures and the full night full of everything. Racks of licorice whips and horehound lollipops. Trusses and decongestant. Tittering motes continually seeking purchase on the surface of products. Tubes of cream and bottles of oils lingered, yellowed and dried out. Fire measles, milk sickness, scrivener's palsy, chilblains, stink damp, quinsy, lumbago, scrumpox, decrepitude. The days passed in this way, the parade of disease and decay, wrinkled humans not long for this world begging to be saved through some salve, but there is neither time nor death, only laughter and variations on light on the surface of things. The women groan in beds, bed sheets flayed. Legs drawn up. Living Waters. Still Waters. Autumn Waters. Pleasant Waters. They sigh and take visitors and call names out to strangers in the hall. And soon, they will be twenty-one, lazing in summer air, lingering in fields, eyes closed. Long legs dipping down into still pond water. A break from working at the telephone company or at the drugstore. Pond water colder than anything against long toes. Soon itchy grass scrapes thighs and goose-fleshed arms. Soon: flat clouds passing above, something inside rumbling like devils caught in a box, and then they will be off elsewhere, younger and younger, holding mother's hand as they watch a house burn, or as they watch a parade end, the marching band's thump fading just beyond the courthouse. And then the music is gone and then a spark of darkness that grows closer, because that was always the first thing anyway.

MRS. SHEPHERD WENT THROUGH THE HOUSE, tore down the curtains, the dark rooms blasted with morning light, the den floor's hardwood gleaming in a parallelogram of sun.

A few nights later, Leah woke to the sound of the back door shutting softly. The faintest click of latch. Nothing but a small metal sound. She was awake, perfectly lucid in the shifting, flat darkness of her room. She listened, hoping the sound she heard was something from the other side of sleep. Some strange dream of doors closing.

Then she heard the first footstep. Her skin roared to life. Prickled and goosefleshed. The pits of her knees and elbows bloomed with perspiration. Her neck and cheeks felt as though they'd been ignited.

The footsteps echoed across the hardwood floor downstairs, slowly. A lumbering darkness. As it neared, she felt the pressure in the room rise, as though it was pushing all the air in the house before it, leaving nothing but void and vacuum behind. Then it was on the stairs, the tell-tale squeak of the third. She did not breathe.

And then it was in the hall. It was just outside of her door. She squeezed her eyes shut, she tried to retreat all of her senses into herself as if it would make her invisible to whatever was in the hallway, just behind the door. She could hear it huffing in the hallway and she began to siren and shrill and she emptied her lungs into the dark of the house and all was light and her parents rushed in, her father first, taking her in his arms and their faces blots in the too-bright light. There was nothing there. Gossamer fog filled the empty street. The night had expired.

"Perhaps it would be best if she stayed with your father for the summer," Mr. Shepherd said.

She knew the man was going to come take her too, and she watched for him everywhere she went, but he never did.

Couldn't it have been Jacob, coming home? Why hadn't she thought that? Because she knew it wasn't. She knew it couldn't be Jacob, but she could not tell her mother that. They continued to look. They continued to talk to men who took notes and television stations sent smiling women by the house with cameras. For a few weeks at least. She knew and she could not tell her father that she knew. She touched her neck and kept quiet as they looked for her brother.

The red barn's red paint was peeling off of gray wood. In it lived two brown horses who neighed and rolled their black eyes like black rocks in an eddy. They swished their tails and gnawed yellow grass tossed from above into metal baskets. The tails went back and forth but the horse bots still tumbled in knots of air and their young clung to the dark hide. She pointed at them and was taken outside.

A keep of foxhounds panting and baying. Treading the gray ground to ruts. They poured the clanking kibble into dented metal bowls in the white sun. It was loud.

Her fingers hurt pulling radishes. They didn't want to come up. In a far corner, under a wide tree on the other side of the fence, a cistern for when the horses were let out. She slapped the surface with her hand. The water was black in the black barrel. The red barn was so far away. Leah thought she'd never make it back. She asked her grandfather if she could go walk down along the stream. Hills, pale yellow with pale grass, swell against afternoon sky and are topped with trees whose bare branches, black against the blue, reach up in rivulets, soil seeping into sky.

Not green bowers so lush they are nearly black with life but the broken body of a bull out beyond the last field. While at work, staring at the empty fields of a spreadsheet, she remembered that summer. A birthmark in the shape of a crab on the side of her neck, a cloud of pigment hidden underneath cascades of crimped hair. In the office bathroom, she sees herself in the mirror after she washes her hands, making sure all is in place and looks at the birthmark. The image in the mirror does not ripple or change like the water barrel. Throughout the day, her hands would flutter to the hair that hung there in that spot and make sure that the dark claws of that unexpected crustacean were obscured. Birds flickered by the window outside. She did not date, though she'd been engaged once. It had not worked out, but it was no tragedy. She hadn't loved him though she tried.

The summer when she was ten, she watched the bull in the pasture, her grandfather by the blue barrel of rainwater, her face baking in the sun. She wandered his farm, crawling over slumping rock walls and under rusted barbed wire, balancing on logs fallen across shallow streams, slipping into the cool shade of a grove, only to be lured home as the shadows got long by his calling her name to supper.

In the mirror at work, she looked fine. She smiled and shut

off the lights and fan as she opened the door. "There was a call for you," the receptionist said, "but he didn't leave a message."

Beyond the trees that lined the stream she found a dead bull upended, neck oblique at roots' maze. She could not imagine how it got there. The sky turned cloudy and she ran home.

The boys sit in the shade of a weeping willow and try to catch crawdads with their bare hands while a man with a cigarette stands on the bridge watching.

"You ain't gonna catch shit like that." He laughs and continues walking. He sits downtown for a while, across from the nonprofit where Leah Shepherd works, hoping to catch sight of her as she comes and goes. He watches the sad-looking women and laughs at their funny walks, laughs at their shrieking children, laughs and coughs. Eventually, he moves on after noticing a middle-aged man in tattered pants staring at him. He walks back by the stream, but the boys are gone. On the cement are the bodies of the crawdads they caught and crushed under their shoes.

Beneath the bushes that lined the fence between the yard and the drive-in, something Leah's seen on the higher channels when her mother was out of town and her father slept. The wide, green leaves aflame with sunlight. The ground aflame with green sunlight. Later by the stream, a boy from youth group thrust his fist into the cold water and shattered it. The look on his face terrified her.

A group of home-schooled children in the cave. Two girls, one deaf, a young boy with a limp who claps at the bats hanging in bunches from damp stone. A young mother watches them linger along, listening to the young woman in shorts describe how deep in the Earth they are. Leah held her grandfather's hand as they ducked below cave bacon.

All of God's trees and grass and sun an eternity above. "These limestone caves prove the Creation Story true. Nothing so vast could have been worn away without the great waves of the Great Flood. Girls? Girls? Listen! Girls!" Her grandfather whispered into her ear: "Bullshit."

In dripping bone, they are close together. A thin mouth, lit by hidden bulbs. Then the young woman turns the lights out and in the perfect dark, the girls roar into nothing.

The endlessly reeling stars on strips of cinder block, pavement brightly lit on a humid summer night, in flickering light, bodies of flies on a window sill. Leah Shepherd walked across the parking lot in the warm night. The mark was not unusually large or dark or odd. It did not cross her mind, not large or dark or odd in any way, but she kept her hair long, but long hair was the style, long hair dangling about the shoulders. Most meals, she ate at chain restaurants on the bypass. Water rises, water falls, water freezes, water melts. Not large or dark or odd. After she ate, she stopped by the department store to pick up a few things.

The girls in the cars of older boys breezing past her grandfather's farm. Leah sat on the porch with the old man, in the dark, in the silence, and she enjoyed it. The young people would pass and he would spit into the dark beyond the porch and utter a soft oath. Walking along the sidewalk when she went into town with him, Leah could see the girls' bare shoulders and she thought of the stillness of the bull. It was dead but seemed to move and she clouded over.

Clean and gleaming aisles of goods. Green plastic buckets perfectly molded, sponges, bleach of every sort, chlorine bleach, oxygen bleach, bleaching powder. She watched the people moving through the aisles. She caught her reflection in the door of the freezer case and was lost for a moment, remembering those passing cars, the cows in the field and the bull in the roots, the blue barrel and her face in it, her grandfather's unbreakable silence and her parents finally coming to take her back home, back to the house where she now had a room to herself, and then exhaling, the moment broken, she looked at the time and walked to the checkout lane and the surface of the blue barrel shattered. She turned, thinking she heard someone calling her name, but no one was there.

Her grandfather's house was a small blue egg in a dirty palm. A blue house at the edge of an orange pasture between low lime hills crowned with bare black trees. Orange pastures and lime hills with gray lines of slave walls, slumping rocks that were cool when she touched them, speckled with yellow lichens and tufts of dark green moss. Walls that were the same gray as the jutting limestone rising from the ground all around the fields, stuttering stones, accidental *menhirs*, worn into existence by rainwater running off of the face of the sun-warmed hills. During the day, the stones cast shadows that didn't mark the passing of much of anything. At night, one or another of these limestone teeth would occasionally align with some distant glowing body, but most of the time they did not, choosing instead to simply point off in a direction that contained nothing all the way until the end.

Leah remembered all of this, though she never talked about it. When she would think about that summer, she remembered that it was warm, but she could not remember what that warmth felt like. She knew that she spent the summer there with her grandfather after Jacob was gone, but those memories felt out of place in the logbook of her life, as though they were extra scenes from some other existence that she'd happened upon. She saw herself from a distance.

Dumb brown beasts wandered about their bounded spaces, heads down, chewing grasses into submission. They bellowed evenings beneath black skies speckled with nameless fires, fires he knew were likely long since lost, cold orbs, empty space, darkness, only their last waves cast down to this house through everything. The bands of light that spilled across the dome above her flickered and warbled like its twin that lived on the surface of the water in the barrels behind the house when she dipped in her hand. Rippling waves destroying the universe. She sipped the cold water from her cupped palm and waited to see how long after her grandfather called her to come in she could linger outside before he'd come looking for her, shouting her name into the darkness. She stood waiting, listening for him to call her name again. She was not thirsty, but she loved to see the still face sent aflutter and the galaxy destroyed.

From the attic window of the farmhouse, an octagon of glass, she could see the fields and trees and hills and rocks swim into one another beneath the prismatic dusk. A confusion in the growing dark. Some nights, when clear, high on far-flung hilltops she could make out other lights, the lights of the other families, and beyond them, against a night's low clouds, the pale light of the small town. At night, the dark was dark beyond dark, dark to the point of being truly void. Even the moon at its most pregnant did little to lift the oozing black. Each cricket's chirp, rather than filling the void with some small movement, only sounded the extent of the emptiness. Day and night there was only the cacophonous roar of nature, a throbbing thrum of insect and animal life chattering like cold teeth on a bone, the clickity-clucking of hard-shelled creepers and segmented crawlers that the mind could not fathom the splendor of, the soprano trilling twitters of bright yellow and red sylvan oddities, the howls of hounds harrowing the valley like a rude blade with a taste for soil. Even the plants, still and detached, made noises: slim rustles and whistles, dry cracks and moans. All a spray of color and scent, sound and warmth rising in tired waves over and over, never ending, never dying, only growing and churning itself back into growth, churning back on the small farmhouse that sat at its center. All of creation fading into one indistinct, luminous mass and she hated everything about it. The leaking sap, the trickling streams, the scampering paws. She sat in that window, looking out into the unlimited darkness, past the few faint lights that marked the edge of the world, and thought of the distant town. The endless plain of light and motion. People pressing against one another. Voices thronging up. Machines and glass. One humming note unable to be noted on any known staff, a note more complex and majestic than anything that Nature ever dreamed of. That town and then beyond, the flickering flecks of the milk strewn across the sky, other suns and rocks and moons and the things that flittered between them the way the cows lumbered between clover and cistern. All spiraling and blinking forever.

One morning, before her grandfather was up, she slipped out of the door, and down the path, toward the trees. In the pale of the moon you could see her, a minnow darting from the porch to the fence, through the rows of corn, hair disappearing, blue dress drained of color, then gone, passed into the woods. When he woke and could not find her, he went outside, hollering for her, dressed only in the long johns he slept in and a hunting jacket that was by the door. He hollered and hollered her name, kicked across the fields, down by the stream, through the trees, and found her sitting on a knot of roots. Relief gave way to a sharp anger, and relief that he'd not called her parents right away. "Leah!" he said. She looked up startled, her face red and wet, and he softened, breathing deep, releasing the hard words that were so quick in him, and he took her hand and lifted her up and dried her face and said, "Why did you do that? I didn't know where you were. Do you know what I thought? Do you know what your parents would have thought? Oh, do you know what that would have done to them?" and she didn't respond, but felt sick to her stomach with shame and anger and some terrible feeling that she did not have the words to name. Later, her grandfather took her out to the far side of the corn, to the edge of the wood. The house invisible from that point. "What, what?" Leah asked, staring at her feet as she walked through the rows, kicking clods. He didn't respond. Then she saw it. The small doe. Brown and white fur flat against shivering body. Black eyes, wet, like cupfuls of water scooped at night. Nose. Tongue. It lay in the sparse green grass at the foot of the wood. She was about to ask her grandfather why it was covered in amaryllis when she realized. The woods heaved with animals that coursed through the woods like silverfish through a library. The doe was still alive. She could feel her heart beating with her eyes. Her grandfather handed her a knife. Heavy, clean. "She's in pain," he said. He held her hand to its wet throat.

And then the summer ended and Leah came home to begin fifth grade at Edna L. Toliver Elementary School.

And now somewhere her little brother was scared, was in pain, was dead, was—

"Leah," her mother said, "Hush. Please, God. Hush. It is time for school."

She didn't know what to expect when she saw her classmates. She'd seen no one she knew since it happened. Several of her classmates' parents had called in the days that followed to offer their support to the Shepherds, and Mrs. Shepherd told Leah that a few of her classmates had called themselves, probably at the prodding of a parent, but Leah hadn't talked to anyone. She'd just been in her room, waiting, certain that at some point her parents would come in, faces red with rage, realizing that this was all her fault, ready to peel her skin off with a belt. She sat in homeroom and waited for the bell and the pledge and the anthem, and her classmates, children she'd been in school with since kindergarten, or before in some cases, filed in and sat in desks as directed by the teacher, a heavyset man with a gray crest of perfectly structured hair, and they talked to one another loudly and they fidgeted and fussed and some fussily put away the new year's supply of paper and glue and some turned and looked at her and then leaned together to whisper. Their whispers scissored through her skin. After morning announcements, they began learning math. At lunch Leah sat alone. Rectangular pizza on soft white bread and a half pint of chocolate milk. At recess, Leah sat on the swings. Then the day ended.

Was something in the house? Her skin prickled, responding to the slightest fluctuation in pressure, a sensitive flame. The skin on the nape of her neck felt warm. The house spoke the sounds that old houses speak: that too-heavy creak on the stair, that groan of door hinge, that rough breath. But no sound came that she could discern from the clutter of sound that comprised the silence of the night.

The smell of machines, of paper and printer ribbon. The men wandered off to waste the day talking about that boy who'd gone missing to anyone who would listen to them. "It just ain't like it used to be. Can't trust none. You see how some of those people are. How they dress. How they talk. Just sad." Lower lips lined with the black shards of the last dip.

In the kitchen, her mother standing over the sink crying in the darkness qualified only by drapes of light from the streetlamp just outside the window. It licked away a few traces of night with hazy warmth. The room was black everywhere save slivers of pale pink-yellow.

Mrs. Shepherd took to reading a verse of the Bible every day and made it as far as Psalm 27. Mr. Shepherd came home from work, ate dinner, put Leah to bed and quietly went back to work. Her mother's mouth moved silently. Her father kept the door to his library closed. The leaves were to turn brilliant colors but it rained and washed them away. Silly birds with a mind for games. And then winter and spring and summer. She did not hear her father come home. Her father went away on a business trip for a few weeks. When he came home, he gave her a stuffed dog. Leah tossed it in the closet. She was too old for such things.

Voices straining to stay unheard. The night sky erupted and the whole house smelled like running water. She sat up and in the passing bright shadows saw her children reading from a book on the floor, turning the pages in the dark. A voice outside, echoing in the street, echoing off houses. The house was quiet. The ground swallowed the rain and was dry again.

Dusty school windows with slants of light. Had anyone seen any faint light moving between the stones and the obelisks? Could even they hear the singing, a faint melody she did not know? The teacher called her name, told her to go to the principal's office where she was excused from school for the rest of the week, the boy suspended. The singing followed her home.

There were birds in the school. Brown-black bodies. Swoop and swirl around the halls, darting high to the exposed beams of the student commons, shitting on anything they could get their shit on. The children would cheer. Small voices and the beating of wings. The custodian would chase them up and down the school with brooms and yardsticks, hollering and whooping, quickly out of breath. Sometimes a dead bird would appear on the floor, a feathered comma in the middle of the gray marbled tile. The children would scream.

The bathrooms were always cold and when in there alone, you could hear soft voices being carried at odd angles from some other place.

"And then judge said, Ma'am do you realize that you are facing felony abduction charges? And then I said, Whatever, it's my birthday. I mean it should be attempted murder. When you are holding someone down and they can't breathe. And something like illegal possession of personal property. I finally got my coat back. See, she likes that Mike's Hard Lemonade. We just sat in the car at the end of the parking lot, it was raining, and we sat and listened to the radio and once she was drunk enough, I took her back to her mother."

Leah kept her eye on the windows of the classrooms on the third floor, the ones no longer used, with orange shades drawn, pale, sun-faded eyelids. She watched for slight movement, a tremble, a twitch, a face looking down.

Leah kept her eye on the street, on passing cars that slowed. Listened for the sound of idling engines. Vans parked discreetly around corners. Men sitting in shade, leaned back, eyes closed. A man in thick glasses with a bald head glistening in morning light watched her come in from the parking lot of the gas station across from the school and Leah was crying as the boys and girls on the swings dared one another to leap off and fly as high as they could. She went shopping with her mother and a man with a thin gray beard touched her head and told Mrs. Shepherd that Leah would be a real heartbreaker one day. A man in the back of the movie theater watched her walk with her father toward the exit as the credits rolled. When would the car stop, the door open, the arms reach out, the voice speaking calmly: *Your mother is sick. Your father is hurt. They asked me to bring you to see them. Come, come, come.* The school offered a program on identifying the danger of strange people. Those that are overfriendly. Those that are threatening. Those who claim to know your parents. Pictures of boys and girls who trusted and disappeared into nothing, never to be seen again. The man who presented the program stopped Leah in the hall and crouched down and said, "You wouldn't ever talk to a stranger, would you?" He smiled and wet his lips with his tongue. And the stories she read in the books she checked out from the public library: children lost in the mists on the moors, hounds the size of horses carrying babies away, a man rushing to confront a noise in an unused room only to return with his hair turned white and his eyes empty and dead. Perhaps there weren't vampires and werewolves and creatures in the lake, but there was something. Leah knew that.

Leah kept her eye on the empty white sky and on a girl's dirty sneakers that hung over the side of the slide, talking to someone else, ignoring Leah completely, they all ignored her at first. A calamity of floral scent from the flowering vines on the fence nearby, the names of which she would never know, trembled. They ignored her at first and then a boy with hair that curled at the nape of his neck hooted at her in the hall. He said, "I'd run away too if I was your brother. I wouldn't want to be the brother of no fat lezzie." And the boys around him howled. They all cackled and clapped and there were girls in pristine Tretorns by lockers covering the grins and the boy said, "You know he's dead. You know that, right? He's probably dead somewhere. Probably covered in maggots, crawling all in and out of his mouth and eye." And then he ran over to her as she stood stricken on the wide tile of the hallway and put his arm around her, "Don't cry, baby. It will be okay. I heard he's haunting the third floor girls' bathroom now. You can see him every time you take a shit." And everyone in the hall died, just absolutely died, and Leah shook and her skin boiled with blood.

On the playground the girls in the bright shoes talked on the slide. "Do you ever think about it? About being dead? About going to heaven or hell? About being trapped, forever, inside a house? A ghost? Do you wonder what it would be like to be forever but to not be alive? That would be terrible, wouldn't it? I mean, to have to be in the school forever? Or to have to live in your house forever and to have to watch your parents cry every night and to have to watch them get old and die and to see new people move in and not care about you or even know you lived there and have to watch people go to the bathroom and sleep together and they can't hear you and it never ends? And what if the house burns down? What happens to you? Do you get to go to heaven then or do you have to haunt an empty lot forever and ever? Haunt a gravel pit? Haunt a grassy path? Haunt a parking lot? That doesn't seem right. I've never heard of a ghost in a parking lot or in a park. I know you think about it. I know you think about him and wonder where he is. I'm sorry. I'm sorry. I know. Wait, listen, wait. Do you ever think—"

One morning, she woke with a pop, like the string on a bow snapping. She sat up and the room was a watery blur. Yelling, she made it down the steps to where her mother was standing in the morning sunlight that came through the high foyer windows. "I think something is wrong," she said. Her eyes were bleeding. She had to go to school for three days with bandages across both eyes. For three days the edges of the whispers in the rooms and halls were sharpened. Every poisoned sibilant and each spiteful plosive expanded to fill the whole of her sensory experience. Rather than listen to the teacher talk about long division and Kentucky history and sedimentary rocks, she heard nothing but a swarm of empty sounds that she was certain were meant for her. After the bandages came off, her eyes were still red for several days and framed by large new glasses, and the boys in line for lunch leaned over and asked if her face was getting its period and then, so proud of themselves, they couldn't even laugh. One boy who'd been held back two years sat next to her during lunch while the other smaller boys watched and he put his hand on her leg and told her that she was really getting nice titties and even the girls laughed, because it was embarrassing to have breasts, and Leah, ashamed to have her body noticed, tried to fold up inside herself. "I saw him," someone shouted and then they would roll back their eyes, and moan a moan that would fill the school's hallway, bright with winter light.

They weren't bad children, were they? They just wanted to carve their names into something while they were still sharp.

———

"—no one is watching us—"

That was her life for the next three years. When she looked back on the time now, Leah didn't remember much. Nothing stood out. She went to school, but there were only about three or four days that she really remembered. That round boy crying and the light on her father's straining neck as he shouted about the call from the school. The day her teacher fell down and broke her leg. The day a boy brought gin to school in a medicine bottle and after drinking it, threw a dull ninja star at the principal's calf. The day there was a fire drill while it snowed. She couldn't remember much at all from those years at home. It was as though they'd never been, days unwritten by whoever was creating her life. She would lie in bed in her one-bedroom apartment and feel the breeze sneak in and slip across her bare legs and she would slowly lower her mind back and back, trying to find something she'd forgotten, but those years were mostly empty. The bright days of Jacob's life outshone everything that came after. The few memories she had of her parents from that time were memories of her mother or father talking to her, or to one another, or to someone else, about Jacob. When she did well in school, her mother would talk about how bright Jacob had been. When she was punished for disobeying her parents, they would often get lost halfway through their reproach, falling into a reverie, remembering some time that Jacob had misbehaved, remembering how mad they'd gotten at him then and become so overwhelmed with regret for what sharp words they'd used with the boy, that they would just walk off, leaving Leah uncertain whether she was still in trouble or not.

Edna L. Toliver Elementary School was a three-story brick building with six granite steps leading up to the wide red front doors, four Doric columns holding the pediment far above the still drowsing heads of sleepy children who wandered in. It had once been the only school, but now was less than half full, the town's young families having ended up in newer houses in newer parts of town, in newer school districts with newer schools. Old tile walls and plaster ceilings with crumbling places where the water got in and wide halls lined with doors into classrooms and pipes that clanged in winter. Windows obscured with dust, but so high the janitorial staff could not reach them to clean. At the center of the old school, a courtyard no one ever used, its doors always locked. Leah Shepherd would look out into it, at the broken fountain and the overgrown grass and imagined it was a cursed place where the cursed bodies of bad children were buried after having died from being paddled.

And on the third floor were locked rooms, unused, with blinds drawn against the sun, rooms full of old student files, out-of-date textbooks, broken desks and broken chalkboards and broken record players. The lights in the hall were always out, the only illumination being from one window at the far end of the hall, a window that faced out into the courtyard. The empty classrooms were dark with dark shades drawn over the windows in the doors.

Any good school of a certain age will be the subject of outlandish tales that are almost certainly untrue. Once, the students of Edna L. Toliver Elementary School shared this tale: The third floor was unused for a reason. Once, years and years ago, there had been a young girl that something terrible happened to. It was just before the school year ended for the summer. The teacher let the students go out to play on the playground but told the young girl that she could not play because she'd done poorly on a test. She had to stay and do some extra lessons. So the whole class went out to play on the playground, which thrilled them because it wasn't even recess time. They flooded out on to the swings and slides. This was before the school built the new playground in the back of the building, the safer playground with soft woodchips and swings with rubber-coated chains. This was the old playground on the side, the remnants of which were still there like the rotten remains of a vanished civilization, and which the current student body was expressly forbidden to play on. Moss covered and overgrown. So these children, blessed with an extra recess swung and played tag and yelled and screamed and eventually the principal of the school, alerted to their presence by the sound of unfettered joy, came rushing out of the school to see what was happening. He asked them what they were doing and where their teacher was and they said he was inside and he let them outside to play. The principal clapped his hands and ordered everyone to return to the school and just as they were leaping from their swings, frowns forming, they heard a terrible shriek from high above them. They looked up to the third floor, their floor, and just at that time they saw the young girl who had been made to stay fly from the open window. She fell, down and down and landed on the cement sidewalk that curled around the school. Blood ran from beneath her in rivers. At that point, everyone began to scream and run toward the door into the school. The principal went to the girl, but it was clearly too late. Inside, the screaming children ran to their classroom, instinctively, only to find within the teacher in a pool of his own blood, dead, slumped in the corner, scissors still protruding from his neck. The screaming increased and others came out of their classrooms to see what had happened. There was no school the next day, but no one took any joy in it. And to this day, no one knows what happened. Some of the young, self-appointed historians passing the story along claimed that the teacher had tried to attack the student and that she had killed him in self-defense and then flung herself from the window out of grief. Some said that the teacher threw the girl from the window in a fit of rage because she could not get the lesson right, for he was a stern teacher, and it was he who killed himself out of guilt. Yet another story claimed that the girl had killed the teacher for no reason and then leapt from the window for no reason other than to thrill at the feeling of falling. But since the summer before Leah's last year of the school, the story had become that the third floor was haunted by the ghost of Jacob Shepherd.

She did not believe in ghosts and certainly did not believe the stories the other students passed around about Jacob haunting the third floor. She could remember the year before when it was still haunted by the dead girl. Plus, Jacob wasn't dead, just missing, so it didn't make any sense to say that he was haunting a place where he didn't die.

Despite knowing better, Leah was still scared of the third floor. Perhaps Jacob did not haunt those halls, perhaps nothing did, but whenever Leah had to go up there on an errand for a teacher, some cold worm wriggled in her mind and she filled with fear. The empty eyes of the gauntlet of doors watching her as she moved down the hall, even without the possibility of the undead, it was too much. There were worse things in this world than spirits and haunts, real things hiding behind doors, watching you through cracks in a shade.

It had been her misfortune for her teacher to ask her to go up to the library and return with a filmstrip. At the top of the stairwell were the heavy old doors that opened into the hall and at the other end were the north double doors of the library. She stood there at the end of the hall and saw nothing but the reflection of the distant light on the ceramic tile. She closed her eyes for a moment, breathed, and then opening her eyes again, began to walk down the hall. For a few feet it was fine, just as always, because nothing ever actually happened. For a few feet it was fine. But then she felt something brush her ankle. She stopped and looked down instinctively, her mind at that moment, too late, thinking 'don't look.' But she did look. Nothing, of course. Just a phantom feeling on young skin. But as she stood in the middle of the wide empty hallway, looking down at her ankles, she heard something behind her. A soft, shrill sound. A squeak. By the stairwell door, the girls' bathroom door opened slowly. Just a little. She stood transfixed, unable to move. The door, a heavy wood fire door like every other door in the old school, swung inward, inward on a dark bathroom. She could see in, but only a short way as the little light from the hallway did not invade that bathroom very far. The light was out. A dark eye opening. She watched, unable to move. The door stopped moving and just at the edge of the gloom, she thought she could see someone standing. A young figure in the faint dark, still, unspeaking and she began to call out, her body flooded with joy and relief, recognizing him even as his face was lost in the light-lessness and she was about to call his name and then she remembered and she knew that it could not be and she stood silent, her mouth open and trying to scream but unable. Abruptly freed of the spell, Leah ran toward the light of the library. She hit the door at full speed, but the doors did not open and she hit her nose on the glass, leaving a streak on the glass and a thin stream of red blood down her lip. The doors were locked and there was a note from the school librarian that said, *Be Right Back.* Leah was trapped. She looked and the door to the bathroom was still open. She could hear something, not from the bathroom this time but in one of the classrooms. A sliding sound. Her whole body shuddered with the slamming of her heart. Then, just as slowly as it opened, the bathroom door began to close. When it shut, with a dull clunk, she ran to the stairwell door, burst through and down the steps, two at a time. On the second-floor landing, she could see out the window onto the side of the school. The morning fog was still full, and illuminated with flecks of morning sunlight. She looked out the window, panting, but even before she looked, she knew what she would see down there on the sidewalk. Someone walking by, a dark shape in the bright fog. The figure paused for a moment, glanced up, and Leah took off running again.

She hadn't seen anything. No ghoulish figure of a long-dead student. No shambling corpse of a long-dead teacher. No spectral lights or disembodied voices. She hadn't seen her brother. That night, replaying the event in her mind, she could only say she saw a door move. The thing was, as she thought about that door, from the safety of her bed, she realized how disappointed she was that she hadn't seen anything else. She wanted to see something. She fell asleep trying to imagine what she could have seen.

But then, the summer before they started high school, her family went to the beach. The following fall, with the help of Judge Whitehead, when he was still just an attorney in private practice, the family petitioned the court to have Jacob officially declared dead. They'd held onto hope and circulated photographs with various advocacy groups and even tried to get some attention on national television, but there wasn't any interest. Then one day, a group of middle school children found a pile of Sunday dress clothes folded up neatly in the attic of an abandoned house just outside of town. There was blood on the shirt and pants. Mr. Shepherd had to go down to the police station and identify the clothes. Leah couldn't sleep that night, hearing her mother's sounds.

But before that, when they still hoped, the family drove to the Outer Banks of North Carolina and they sat on the sand. Mr. Shepherd walked to the pier and looked at the rising dark and listened to the waves break.

Flickers of ocean air in morning light. A girl was on the beach, out on the shore playing in the surf. Tall stalks of grass topped the sandy banks and the wind spoke through them. Years later, in bed in the apartment complex, with her window open and listening to the breeze breathing through the new leaves on the nearby trees, Leah remembered the voice of the wind in the tall grass on the dunes and she wondered if it was the same voice, saying the same thing. It had been her family's first beach trip without her brother. Her mother sat inside with a book, but didn't read, her eyes sat on the words and waited. They kept saying that this trip was just what they needed. Her father walked along the shore alone, trying to get to the distant pier, but always turning around before he reached it. "It never seems to get closer."

She thought of the wind in the tall grass, there in the full-size bed in the one-bedroom apartment of her adulthood, and she thought about the girl playing, wet red hair, skin was already burning—pale flesh sprinkled with cinnamon. Mirrors rimmed in rope, dried starfish and scallop shell. She walked down to the water and saw the girl was sitting right at the edge, tossing her head to the side as the waves broke on her body. Her oval face covered in freckles. An upside-down mouth. Her father asked her to walk with him and she watched as their footprints faded behind them with each tongue of water, watched the pier resist their advance, and when they returned, the girl was gone.

One night, she walked with her father to the pier. There was an arcade on the boardwalk and Mr. Shepherd gave Leah some quarters and left her at the bright door as he walked down the pier alone. Inside, the light was plagued by flapping wings and the air swirled with the sounds of failed levels and a group of boys in shorts, without shirts, began to hoot at her. One leaned in and began to sniff her hair while his friends howled. "I'd fuck her," and then laughter and, "You're sick, man." Leah became afraid to be alone in that noisy room, even though there were dozens and dozens of children and teenagers milling around, leaning into the electric boxes, watching one another play, and she ran out and down the pier looking for her father. The pier was dark, illuminated only by a few lamps on high poles. There were a few people on the wet wood hunched over their tackle boxes or buckets of fish guts, cleaning up and getting ready to go home. She kept seeing men standing in the shadows and thinking they were her father only to find, just as she was close to them, that they were strangers, leaning on the railings, looking at the stars above or back at the glowing windows of the condos on the shore. At the very end she found her father and as she ran to him, she realized he was making a strange sound and she stopped. He heard her approach and turned to the sound, unsure who was running up to him, and he saw his daughter. She could not see the look on his face. She could not tell what he was doing. "Honey, why are you—" but he stopped and seeing that she was crying, he leaned down and hugged her, though she was getting close to being as tall as he was at this point, and in the faint light she could see his wet face and realized he'd been crying as well. He held his daughter and Leah realized that in all those years, she'd never seen her father cry for Jacob. The weight of the loss had been written on him daily, but she'd never seen him lose control and as he held her, she also realized that he must think that she was crying for the same reason and she felt a quiver of guilt that she'd found something else to cry about.

In her office, a gap in the old window whistled with cold gusts and she listened, trying to understand what it was whispering.

She pulled the chain on the light, casting bolts of darkness across the room. The blood ran in her. She stood at the window, and the softly lit parking lot danced in vague patterns. The trees were rattling and there was nothing in Heaven or Hell that could change that.

The slap of her shoes across the wet parking lot. The roar of rain waking her at some point in the well of night. A sound in the hall—her mother? Her father? The old creature with long claws she used to threaten Jacob with to make him settle down and let her sleep? The girl, having slipped out and crossed the cemetery? And then dawn.

Her first summer job, the pool snack bar. The little room was filled with the scent of searing meat in swirling spires and the buzz of black flies busying themselves along the grease-grimed screen. Drinks bubbled in styrofoam cups and ice melted on tongues and napes. Leah caught sight of Jacob out of the corner of her eye, running across the hot cement, yelling with the other boys, still five. She stopped, looked back, but it was only some other child, ruddy and wet and keening for his mother because he fell down and had cherries on his knees. Her heart raced. She glared at him and hoped he hurt.

That evening, she heard her mother in the hall and pretended to be asleep.

That summer, the summer when she was sixteen, Leah Shepherd made a friend, a girl visiting her grandparents in Crow Station for the summer, lying out by the pool as Leah sweated in the small room, swatting flies and giving golfers watered down sweet tea.

At night, a thin cacophony of the dark rustles in through the windows. Sheets of cloud pass across the illuminated night sky and make the dim light in the room shift. The dark bloom of night sounds. She called and they talked on the telephone. One weekend, they drove to Cave City to see Kentucky's oldest wax museum. On the side of the roads were shacks with card tables of geodes for their consideration. In the 3D Haunted Maze, they clung together and minnowed. In the grass beyond the crumbling parking lot sat a discarded sink with green blades growing in its white bowl. They sat next to it as the sun set. The girl drove a Rabbit with ripped seats and a cassette caught in the player, the wheels ever whining. A sudden downpour caught them. An evening purple amongst monuments. The girl didn't know Jacob or Leah or her family. They didn't talk about anything important. Leah listened to the girl tell stories about her home in Pennsylvania. An evening darting in the pooling shadows of faraway firs. In the distance, the girl's house flickered where her mother and father and sisters slept. She looked at the girl and the pooling shadows and the long purple stains cast by statues in security lights. Plastic flowers foxtrot in the wind. Silk petals rub and rasp.

The screen displayed a gray and black image, dimly lit and impenetrable for a moment, a complex harmony of flickering shadow resisting resolution into anything specific until her eyes were able to decipher the shapes into something meaningful. Static like mist along low grass, along blacktop, black fading into black, the back of the school, a long brick wall, dusty windows, a short cement step and an alcove for a door, dark with security light pooling around. The television makes only one sound, the soft hum of light. Nothing for a moment, then light rising against the wall, the wall washing out, and then cutting off, a car arriving just out of the frame and then two figures slowly, idly approaching the alcove, sitting on the cement step, half in and half out of the darkness…it is summer, the summer passed, the girls, the two pairs of legs in jeans cut off at the knee and pegged, the loose t-shirts, one with hair pulled back in a ponytail, the other with hair cropped short, it is days before one would move away with her sisters, a warm summer night, a night still hot no matter how dark, it is summer and them sitting in and out of the dark, moving further back in the alcove, into the dark, but never disappearing, it is summer and in oceans children call names and cough water and in woods they mark trees to return home and at night they move silent through backyards, leaping from shadow to shadow, seeking to be shadows, nothing more, the parts of the Earth cut from the dominion of light, it is summer and the girls move in to each other, blending and joining, moving hands out of sight, only the tangle of tones of gray, the film silent and gray and black and jittering and then stopped.

At the funeral. "Listen, now is the time. Now we invest. I know you have some money saved up. Listen, listen, I will provide the labor. Listen, do you want a drink? Listen, just a sip? We can buy. We can buy and then reinvest. Listen, do you want some of this or not?" A gallery of chins. A swell of coughing voices. The preacher begins to preach and gets it all wrong.

Pouring out sugar and salt and crying for more soda. "Underneath mountains are giants buried long before any of us were even thought about in God's mind. If you took to mind to move a big hunk of water with your two palms pushed outward—" Children like paper falling.

She watched gutters, toothed with ice or bearded with leaves in flame. And the yellow grass of the yard that she watched her mother mow. She watched the viaduct. Names bloomed underneath and faded with the years. A cut of sky, the gray and blue.

There was a playground on the side of the old elementary school that was never used, but the swings swung in the shade of still maples. She watched the windows. *Can you hear the howling?* The perfect place to perch on a summer night and not be seen.

She walked all over town, watching her own warped self reflected in the windows of the empty department stores. In Constitution Square, two men held hands forever as the circles of governors watch. The log cabins stood empty, their wood walls tattooed with names by knives. There was a walled garden behind the apothecary.

The Shakers built two houses in one house. Two houses to keep the boys and girls apart. Two houses to divide the bodies to enrich the spirit. And work. And toil. And bodies given to the enthusiasm of true spirit. A divided room for dances. All the old hymns that she now sung. And the grass grew and grew and here she found old Easter eggs still hidden in the half of the closet that had been Jacob's.

The girl calls and they fight. Over what? Nothing that either could reckon. The next day, the girl didn't call and Leah walked to her grandparents' house and she found the girl on the deck, reading and they sat uncomfortably for a while and then half-forgot what they were fighting about and went for a drive around the country, but didn't say much of anything at all. The only friend she'd made. The girl's sisters were bright shadows like older siblings always are.

Derrick Green asked her what high school was like and she said, "I can't remember."

The house abandoned at the far end of the field. They approach on foot by starlight, skirting lowing blobs. Word was the house was haunted. Of course it would be. How could it not? Collapsing porch. Empty and slumping. A rotting tooth from some other time. A fine old home at the end of a long lane that must have been owned by a wealthy family but which now sat empty, slipping to seed at the far end of a cow pasture.

A piano in an empty salon and nothing else. Broken glass glittered in the beams of small flashlights. Light steps on worn wooden floor. All silent but their breathing and heart-beating. Written on the walls were the names of bands no one remembered and loves long since lost, fallen to some ruin. Nothing but tears on a car's seat covers.

Leah went to play the piano, but couldn't bear to hear the sound it made. She heard the girl upstairs walking around, she stopped playing the piano, thought about what she'd written earlier, played a chord, listened for footsteps.

The girl's grandparents were doting lumps in synthetic fibers. The girl grabbed Leah's hair and told her that she thought it was terribly cute and that she wanted to cut hers all off as well, but she never did. Leah liked that the girl did not look at her the way that nearly everyone else in Crow Station did. To the girl, Leah was just another friend, a temporary summer friend. Another nobody. Yet, something in Leah made her want to tell the girl all about Jacob, about the reflecting pool, about the boys, about what Leah heard, the voice calling her name, what she never told anyone. Leah wanted to shout it at the girl as the girl was stuffing her pockets with candy and coolly walking out of a gas station.

Leah wanted to crack the cement in her throat and scream, *I have secrets too and they are worse than a pocket of candy.*

That woman woke before the purple night became blue, beneath the bones of branches black and cross-hatched, the damp ground was soft. Quills of unmown grass. That stream ran. The stream that ran through town. That ran from the top edge of town down through and out the bottom. The brown water gushing along moss-browned rock, sun-bleached bottles, crushed cans, overturned clothes washers, avocado green, rusted out, worn, crumbling, washing away in red rivulets in the brown water of the stream. Lifting up, crackling awake, jeans soft with dew, palms pressed out into earth, rising again. A few bare roots, her bag leaned against a trunk. Folded in folds of roots. She crouched at the stream's slippery lip, leaned. Hands cupped. Two pools. A face shivering. She shivered. Several faces. For a moment she could see herself without knowing herself, raw and bare, and she licked dried sweat from the corner of her mouth. Hers in the pools and the wriggling of muscles in her back. The confusion of birds' throats. Water waking up. Pulled from a plastic container her makeup and a mirror and put on her face. Cars passing on the street just beyond the break of trees. Wading out, toe and then ankle and then shin deep, but no more, for a moment bare, stretching bare arms and bare chest and bare legs with aching knees and crouching again as the brown water buffets her brown body and splashing water and fresh gashes and cracked skin and then into gray jeans and sweatshirt and everything else into her bag, just in case and up the embankment by the overpass where the cars pass. *Crow Station Antique Mall.* Shuttered. Cluttered. Dusty window and faded Confederate Flag. *No Trespassing Property of the CSA.* Wooden cross and brass cross and praying porcelain figurine. A school bus half empty with children from the Christian Home and their faces grace the panes as the yellow beast bustles past, gawking down as she soldiers along. A dip and over a curb and down beneath the viaduct to cross the tracks to the abandoned train station. Bricks in crumbling green and red with loose mortar. Men along the lip of the loading dock of the candy warehouse, taking a break watch her wander. Spit from soft chin. Chuck chuck. Rumble above and the walls creeping with fading names. Slices of howls, howls through her sweatshirt. Howls through her skin. Howls settling in. A group of men clamored her face, but she pulled out of the howl and kept along the sidewalk by the old house cut to pieces with the cluster of plastic things along the dirt yard. A man from church her mother brought to talk to her had howled out from within her and the man her mother married had howled and she kept those too, but the first one had been so distant, its own voice was lost in the chorus of them howling. The old buildings, the paths of the college, the young milling and darting. The young in tangles. Clumps. Weaving. A girl's French braid amiss, strands threaded wrong, hairs pulled apart, out and tangled. The braid ruined from being rolled on. The arms in legs in arms and arms. The lithe writing. Forgetting. Cars and cars and they looked but those that passed on foot found interest in the gutter. She stomped and stepped and waited at the crosswalks to pass. The passing booms of bass. The petals of treble. The muffled words. The courthouse looms behind the garden. The bell tower. Hands. Long black. Nearly pointing to God. She sat on a bench and rested and watched the people pass. Men in suits. Women in suits. Men in pickup trucks and white vans. Women in skirts and sweatpants with children gaggling along. Young women with long hair and long denim skirts, hair covered. Young men with long necks angled awkwardly. Chins covered in black or blond hair. Lips with downy coating. Goslings. Young women in tight jeans, clutching curves of hips. In yellow jackets with fur-lined hoods. The young with hands to their faces, speaking into their palms. Men and women looking down into their palms. Looking down and flitting fingers skating along. A woman in a floral dress floated with two men behind her. One in a suit. The other in overalls. Comb-over, bearded. The woman looked ahead, but her eyes were elsewhere. She floated. The men trudged. The man in the suit slumped and shivered. The man in the overalls rolled. They went in and by the fountain where the town's children's pennies constellated, a young man in a black shirt and black jeans set up an empty bucket and a small amplifier and began to sound the Word. And then along the street, Romans on sign and pillars of marble. BAPTIST CHVRCH. Porticos. Verandas. Ivy. Maple. Holly. Oak. Elm. Blue. White. Brick and brick. Bones of the Earth. The smell of woodstove and exhaust. Sedans pulling from drive, pausing to look at the passing cars and sliding out into the stream and they paused to watch as she stood, waiting for them to be gone, the men with moustaches and without. Bending over. Craning. Growling in the rustling dark. The dark quailed. Had the howling been there at birth or had it been left in her. She was the dark. When there was nothing, it was just her. Weak billowing clouds. Gray sky rumpled like a quilt cast aside. The street ended at the gates of the cemetery.

She listened to the voices as she passed. The voices were on the wind and she listened. Leah Shepherd, on her way to work, sees the woman entering the wrought iron gates of the cemetery. What was that woman's morning like? Did she live in the woods? Leah never went into the cemetery.

A cluster of nine girls stand in variations on a single theme: waiting. Green frocks and purple leggings and jeans and white blouses and hair pulled up, let down, tied, bound, and askew. Their heads bowed, looking down into glowing hands. In front of the new All You Can Eat Buffet, a Mercury driven by a melted old man lets out three old women and then rolls along looking for a parking spot. By the double doors to the buffet, they await his return, clutch purses to ample chests. Point fingers at one another. A young man in red shirt and red pants darts from the office supply store toward his car. Eyes heavy-lidded and hair a black nest. Stocking flat-screens and video game consoles all day and now a break, fingers fumbling for keys so he can sit in his car and pull from beneath the seat one perfect joint.

Black metal blast beats bleat beneath guitars. A major to F sharp minor, tremolo picked. Teenage car songs, teenage love songs, teenage death songs, teenage sex songs. A major to F sharp minor, again and again, no matter how blasted the beats, or how guttural the howls. Pop songs for sad youth. Nearly hitting the woman standing by the guardrail, looking down the embankment.

An anvil crests the trees, late afternoon's black curtain, and as the rain comes, the girls are gone, the women are gone, the songs have stopped.

"What gives you the right to put your hands in my son's mouth, unless he is choking. That is private."

"I can't tell if these diseases are the same or different. Lord have mercy."

Three children stood outside at the window watching. One gnawed a fist. A woman sighed into her cell phone about a still born baby's birth.

"You think I have sass? You should meet my little sister. Her first text was 'Fuck you.' She's a sweetie. I'm not as girly as my sister. She wears tiny tutu skirts. I mean, she's a slut. My brother brought a girl home freshman year but she was like a cow and we gave him shit and he doesn't talk about girls anymore. My whole family makes fun of each other's boyfriends. My dad is very open about his girlfriends."

Leah walked to her car across the parking lot and looked up at the sound of a car bleating and saw that worn-looking woman walking by, along the guard rail. Leah asked a few of the women at work about her. Leah said, "Do you know anything about that woman that just walks around town?" but as soon as she said it, she realized that 'walk' wasn't the right word. It was too casual. This woman was focused. She moved as though compelled by some singular purpose which was beyond Leah's understanding. The right word was beyond Leah's grasp as well. Only a couple people knew whom she was talking about. One person said that the woman used to work at a fast food restaurant or maybe at the department store. "Have you ever seen her nails? They are perfectly done." Another person said that they'd heard that the woman had once been raped, maybe even multiple times, and that she put all that makeup on and walked around like that to look crazy so people would leave her alone. As she passed the woman in her car, pulling out of the shopping center parking lot, Leah considered slowing and offering her a ride, asking her if she needed anything, asking if she would like to come by the nonprofit to see if there was anything they could do for her, but Leah didn't.

On the sidewalk, a card table with fresh tomatoes on it. A woman in a spaghetti-strap shirt and short green shorts feels fresh fruit and shouts to an elderly woman behind the wheel of a turquoise Nissan. Tinted windows, child in the backseat, playing with an empty soda pop bottle.

A boy sings from behind bushes and falls silent.

"Could someone walk me to the church?" a blind man asks. "Can I have your elbow?" He taps his cane and creates the world.

Taps, but does not move. Someone approaches and places the blind man's hand on an elbow and leads the way, but the person does not speak. At the steps of the church, the person walks away.

The young singer takes up his song again. The turquoise Nissan is gone.

The boy told that when his family moved into the blue house on the corner, they found a room in the basement hidden by a bookcase. In the room was a rusted dagger with a leather-covered handle and painted on the wall images he would not describe. "I mean, just like weird stuff," he told, "sick and perverted stuff." Everyone nodded as it had the ring of truth. Across the street from the blue house was a Victorian where a minister lived until his death and then a young family with three daughters. The family was up from Florida. The girls told that their house was haunted. Lights cut off. Plates poured from cupboards in arcs. The youngest heard the voices of men arguing in the fireplace. Behind a brick they found a note written in an illegible hand, written in code, written backward. Obscure and spoiled by time. No one ever saw the note. Everyone waited for the girls to bring it to school, but they never remembered. No one ever saw the ruin of plates. No one ever saw the lights flicker, dim, die. You could hear their father, voice bruising, if you walked by the Victorian on a spring afternoon. After the divorce, the mother moved with the girls back to Florida, but not before the middle daughter became engaged to a libertarian college student from Alabama. The boy in the blue house told this too: Sometimes he could see the girls. Through windows. In their house. "I am Christian, though," he says. "I just want to pray for them." He never showed anyone the secret room. His parents, having said a prayer, sealed it up.

When Leah Shepherd got the car, which had been cheap and was old and every year cost more to maintain than it was worth, she showed her parents, expecting that they would see and understand and turn and look at her and see her and that they would all get in it and drive to the beach together, like they used to do, or even just around town and they would reminisce, and she drove up and leapt out of the car and ran inside and said, "You have to come see my new car," and her mother and father looked at it in the drive and smiled distractedly and shrugged. She wanted them to understand without her having to tell them.

Everyone told her that she needed to get rid of the thing and get something more reliable and with better gas mileage and less blue, but she didn't listen.

Lightning cracks and the world is static. Night, the night yard, the faraway street light.

Scrambled eggs, sausage links, glistening carafes of milk. A gleam of grease in the faint light. Silver platters of food clanging loudly on the hardwood floor. Laughter. Great links of meat.

Mirrors made them soldiers in a chaotic but clockwork army—writhing on lances, crawling along the ground. The smell of cooling sausage patties and warming shrimp cocktails waft in intermittent waves on the whims of the air conditioner that groans loudly over the pulsing mechanical beats. He drove the next morning from Graham, North Carolina, to Crow Station, Kentucky. When he closed his eyes, he could still see the waves of women dancing and the light on their dimpled skin and smell of the wet dumpster he'd parked beside to spend the night.

The man in the door of the motel room by the train tracks raises the half-exhausted cigarette to his lips, the tip of which contains a bright carbuncle that flashes as he breathes in, and looks at the variegated pools on the wet surface of the road where it has just rained.

The men digging the grave for Saturday's service talked quietly as the sun began to set.

"Remember that boy went missing back, I don't know, thirty-some years ago. In the eighties?"

"No."

"I wonder if they ever found out what happened to him."

A shrug.

"I'll tell you, it's like I say, it's got so that you can't trust no one no more. I mean, used to be, children could go outside alone, go all over, you know. But not now. My momma used to send me clear across town to my uncle's house and there weren't nothing to be afraid of."

Dogs marked gates. Starlings clouded. The sound of metal on earth.

"You don't remember that? I still think about that family some. I mean, my boy, he's had his troubles, but at least I can go visit him on weekends."

The other man thought for a moment, shrugged, and told a story about a girl he knew who liked to do it and have people watch. The man recounted the story and they stood, leaning on their shovels.

"A prayer for a husband to get more hours of work. A prayer for a granddaughter who has to have knee and feet surgery. A prayer for a husband to be convicted of using profanity. A prayer for a daughter struggling with depression and mental illness. A prayer for a son addicted to pornography and cartoons. A prayer for a wife to learn to enjoy the work she has been blessed with. A prayer for a daughter to not feel resentment about having to leave her job and help her mother care for her disabled sister. A prayer for a baby to be born. A prayer for an ex-son-in-law to concede on how to raise a child. A prayer for a mother-in-law to see the good in her daughter-in-law. A prayer for a child to stop sassing." And then a swell of strings and commercial break.

In the motel room, he tried to remember what he was going to say. He tried to remember what it was like to be a little boy. What could he say? In the mirror, he watched his lips move, but made no sound. There was someone next door he never saw.

"So after that, he wanted to go over to Western Steer. So we went and an hour became five, can you believe that, five hours and we had these Jell-O shots, or maybe we'd already had those and we just had beer, but lord, lord, lord five hours. It should have been over and she was with us the whole time, pregnant, you know, just big, just about to burst and all I could think about were the Jell-O shots and how I shouldn't have, you know, just shouldn't have. And then I don't even know whose house it was we ended up at, but, you know, it didn't matter at that point and she was just on him, riding, all night, her mouth going so fast, and I seriously thought about sleeping in a ditch or something just because at that point, when we were in the house, whoever's house it was, I was just like, you know, ready to be done with everything, baby or no baby or whatever."

The young couple in their first home marveled at the two raccoons in the moonlight of the backyard. The young couple could not conceive that there would ever be a time when they would not be in their house watching raccoons through the kitchen window. There had been one raccoon on the deck, eating the cat's food, and when it registered some motion from inside the house, the young man putting his arm around his young wife, it ran down into the yard, pausing for a moment to make a sound and the second raccoon ran out of the darkness and together they trundled off. To the young couple, this moment felt as though it would exist forever, this life they had, and even when he sat by her bedside in the hospital, slipping in and out of herself, looking much changed without her teeth, he felt as though all he had to do was to rise from the chair and look out of the hospital window, steadying himself on the sill so he wouldn't slip again, to see those two dark creatures who had long since returned to the generalized life of the Earth.

"You have to see it."

"Wait, wait. Tell me again what you saw."

"Listen. Okay, so I was walking through that one field behind Indian Hills, you know?"

"Yeah, where the Old Country Club is."

"Yes, but I was past that, I cut through the field, passed the old pool, through the trees, down the hill to Clark's Run, and I followed it for a while. I was just killing my day, right. I had on my Walkman."

"What were you listening to?"

"DJ Screw. But wait, listen: so I walk along and I come to this one part where it gets wide and calm. It is totally quiet. Then I come around this bend and it was real quiet and that is when I saw it." He tried to explain what he saw, but the incomprehension on his friend's face silenced him. So they went, cutting across the same fields in the same place, but there was nothing there.

"I don't know. Maybe I was wrong or something."

"This is like that time you tried to get me to go into some cave you found because you said there were some clothes or something."

"Now that, my friend, was true. I totally did. I found this cave and inside there was a little shirt and pair of pants and saddle oxfords placed on top of it like they were placed out by a mother. There were other things, too, like—"

They walked on, trudging through mud and muck. They turned a bend and saw a bull upside-down in the branches of a tree. A perfect, pristine bull, legs like columns in the air.

"Once, I fucked this girl. After we did it, we were laying there and she started to tell me about when she was a little girl visiting her grandfather's farm. It wasn't a big farm. He had a few cows, grew some corn. The usual. Out in the pasture there was a pond. Kidney bean shaped. That's how she described it. Kidney bean shaped. She told me that one winter the pond froze over and a cow tried to walk out across it but the ice was thin and the cow fell through, or part way through. The hind and udders stuck up through the ice, but there wasn't anything that her grandfather could do about it. They couldn't go out on the ice and get it or they would fall through, so they had to wait until spring. When spring came the cows hind and udders began to grow green with moss and small white flowers. I don't know why she told me that while we were flopped there. Her mouth smelled like cinnamon."

The stars offered no solution.

One of the security guards at the hospital died. A young guy, just out of high school. He'd always wanted to be a police officer and he took criminal justice classes in the morning at the community college and worked the graveyard security shift, watching the halls through the night, making rounds of the rambling building on the hour. One morning, a custodian found the young man's body sprawled on the tiles in the maternity ward.

Then, just as people were beginning to move on, one of the nurses went out on maternity leave and gave birth to a baby that everyone heard was 'different' though no further description was given. There was much hushed discussion of 'the poor thing.' All mentions of the baby's name were followed by 'bless its heart.' In any case, the nurse never came back to work.

Soon after that, after the first of summer, the boy went missing and the newspaper was full and everyone had something to think about for a while.

The restaurant's name taped to the window in sun-bleached, bubble letters. The wall behind the cash register encrusted by dusty family photos in tarnished tin frames. Card tables covered in butcher paper. Handwritten menu with Bible verses. The warm smell of frying wafted like cat hair on an updraft. Swirling tendrils of hot dog and chili and hamburger and french fries. Mouthwatering haints of unhealthy desire. The owner watched through the window, hoping the filthy woman walking toward the door, her face caked with colors, was not about to enter and ask for food like the men do sometimes, hats in hand, hairy faces downcast, playing a part. Luckily, the woman, striding in her filthy sweatpants, knees and seat stained with what the owner hoped was mud, battered backpack slung over slumping shoulder, just walked on past the window and the owner felt tension that she did not even realize she was feeling release. She turned and watched the men at the table in suits chewing and staring at the young woman waiting on another table.

"Listen, they drive by real slow. Listen, there are lights outside all night. Listen, there are wires under the ground they put. I know that: They try to take my land, they stand in my road. All twenty of them held me down. God just don't do stuff like that. The Earth is just the Earth. Look me in the eye and tell me how them waggertails got in the bucket then?"

In that last moment, the brilliant catacombs of space, the gathering light. The girl in the purple dress is a parasol. She held out her hand, cupped, ready to catch rain. The streets were half clusters of disappearance. Half clusters of broken wives.

The girl took Leah by the hand and they crawled over the fence. Cheeks and shoulders dotted with drying salt-sweat. Flickering eyelid of a deer, the pink tongue of a toad, the mirror of sound. Beneath a pregnant galactic vista, an eternity of pauses, never more than a sheet drawn across the sun. Fallen trunks of trees, hollow and rotten and some boys that the girl met at the movie theater. Leah leaned forward and she breathed hot breath and saliva back and forth with a boy from another county while a few feet away the girl watched and laughed, having dared her. The air was in bloom with the splendid riot of the bright green cow shit that surrounded them. On the other side of the pasture, the slumping wall, dry stacks of stone and beyond that, the Old Country Club. Air licked the thin blades of dry grass. The boy hooted. Leah felt like weeping, but kept thinking of the girl watching. This or another Sunday of doing nothing but watching Hayley Mills movies in the living room while her mother slept on the couch. She never made it to the Old Country Club to read the graffiti. Never beyond even that, to the sunken stream, blocked from sight by a break of trees, crackling water full of garbage and shaded forever. Hayley Mills looked at her, but she could not hear.

The girl opened the door of an abandoned building and Leah followed. The girl had an empty water bottle of bourbon in her coat pocket. The hall was nearly completely dark. The only light came in from a window at the farthest end from the stairs. They didn't hear anyone and there were no lights on in any of the rooms that they could see, but then, they could hear singing in the dark, but too faint to name. They realized someone was sitting in the dark. The thought, happened upon at the same moment by both, was too much and rather than sneak out, they bolted for the stairs, hit the door with a clatter, and tumbled down the steps like marbles. It was only when they were outside on the empty Crow Station streets that they laughed, a torrent of laughter that neither could suppress.

On her back, stretched on a fallen tree trunk, listening to the clatter of water over rocks, alone, Leah stared up into the now green canopy of trees in the woods where she'd wandered, across empty fields and past the ruins of old farmhouses and the Old Country Club. She matched her breath to the lapping and the crackle of decaying undergrowth and felt her eyes dry out. One of the still standing spires of the decaying clubhouse cluttered with sunlight in the distance. She had nothing planned for the rest of her life beyond this. A warm breeze passed through everything, through her. She could feel the rotting bark scraping her bare calves.

Her neat desk, the case files and the telephone and the cheap toy car that she kept by the computer monitor that looked just like her car.

The telephone rang, but she let it go to voicemail. On her wall hung a framed copy of the article about her from last week's newspaper. The women in the office had given it to her as a gift. The telephone rang but the person left no message.

The wind blew and caused dry leaves to whisper and she was walking along the bank of the stream that ran through the trees by her apartment complex. A black snake hurried from her path, startled and running away like water.

She remembered: They were cutting through a pasture, slipping down between trees to the stream and there had been a snake, green mud and mossy rock. The girl laughed and they took after it. The snake, caught in a crotch of roots. They tossed rocks, laughing, until it was dead, and then something moved through the trees and they, without a word, ran home.

The summer days grew shorter.

They lay in the grass, the green blades rising above them like spires or green teeth in a blue mouth. Leah felt her legs sink into the soil and her friend told her incredibly strange and unbelievable things about Pennsylvania and about her family, most of which Leah had a hard time believing. All mired in the blue around her and smelling the salty smell of the clouds.

That night Leah looked at her own face in the bathroom mirror after her bath, below the bright light of bare bulbs. She looked at her neck, pulling the hair aside. The faint shape almost looked like something. A figure moving through fog, nearly resolving into something she could name, but always elusive.

Grass uncut and ankle high. Sirens, chirping sparrows and cardinals, gutter-tongued hollers of children in distant neighborhoods playing in the street. The deep-earth thrum of hundreds of lawnmowers. The scent of gasoline and billowing grass fills lungs. Spores that cling to legs, arms, and eyelashes. Clusters of dandelion seed taking to sky like infant spiders. The opening eye, the black eye, the widening iris.

But each letter can have a meaning of its own. They can be rearranged to make other names with other secret meanings. Certain letters in a certain order can bring people to life from lifeless garbage. The man showed the child in the parking lot of the motel some of the things he'd cut free from the wood.

As stars cooled and dust became the Earth and as the Earth cracked and became towns and as this town divided and divided again and became his house and his neighborhood, the entire history of life deeper than living is written in him.

Leah looked at her friend's flushed face. Dew dried on lip. The edges of a small pool in the depression of her throat crackled as the warm sun peaked over the soft knoll. Her skirt was bunched around her knees, her left leg bare against the cool shifting grass, kicked out to the side. The left arm lay against her breast, the wrist dangling limp.

There was ink on her fingers. They were quiet. Her legs bled green turf below her, upon her, so that she could be nothing more than graying spores in the crevices in the white paint on the swing, still in the breeze.

"It's not your fault," her friend said.

"But, listen, it is," Leah said. "I never told anyone, but—" There was a knock at the door.

The interior halls of the church were dark, lightless but for the small all-glass walk-way in the front of the church that led to the sanctuary where moonlight and streetlamps cast half-hearted colors. The lock-in's young legs course full speed, slicing through darkness. Heaving lungs power startled cries. Screams melt to laughter. Arms swing pillow cases willy-nilly. Hands brush against anonymous body parts. The faint scent of wintergreen gum and hairspray fills dilated nostrils. They stumble upon two bodies in the dark and a moment of confusion and a gasp and the sound of clothes being quickly rearranged. A soft squeal. The voices of two other girls. Only the faintest light from a distant EXIT sign which revealed nothing.

The children in the children's choir huddled and whispered

and giggled and swooned over one another and turned their back on those that could not sing. "I know a scary story," one of the boys said, but no one listened. "Hey, I know a story and it is true." He just started talking, and they started listening because it was past midnight and there wasn't anything else to do. "So, this friend of mine, this happened to her dad. He's like a farmer and when he was young he got back from Vietnam and his friends told him about this house out in the county. Anyway, he drove around the country roads for a long time, way out almost to Gravel Switch, way out in the boonies. It's by this old cemetery on a hill. It used to be a church cemetery, but a long time ago the church got burned down. No one knows why and they never rebuilt it but you can still see the gravestones. I've been by it. It's real creepy. So, okay, so he went and parked and walked across a field to the house. Oh, so I should say that the man who built the house was insane. He had three girls and he kept them locked in the attic. His wife was dead. She had a disease that made her skin peel off. He was a religious maniac and finally he killed the girls. Maybe he burned the church too. I don't know. But I do know that he stabbed them to death." The boy made stabbing motions and a squishing sound with his mouth which made everyone laugh, but a nervous laugh. "That shit didn't happen."

"No, really it did. My dad told me about that part. He has a copy of the newspaper that told about it. So, my friend's dad crossed the field and it was real dark when he went, but he found the house and there was a full moon and you could see the tomb-stones on the hill, so he gets to the house and it's really tall and kind of leaning over sort of like it's sinking and he pushes the door open." His voice withdraws, softens, very gradually, and slowing down. He lets each word out like a step on hardwood above you in a house that should be empty. He leans forward as does everyone else so they can hear. "So he looks around the house and there is a piano in the parlor with broken keys and in the kitchen there is a black stain on the floor. He had a flashlight that he brought back from the war and he ran the light over the walls. The paper was peeling off and the plaster was bubbling and ruined and rumbling and black in places from mold. He goes upstairs. One step at a time. Slowly. Upstairs there are three rooms and they are all empty mostly, except for one room has a girl's dress hanging in the closet, a white dress, and another room has a stuffed bear in it with the button eyes ripped off of it and then in the last room there is a Bible. He walks over to it to pick it up and he can see there is a nail through it, nailing it to the floor. But that's not the weird thing. The weird thing he notices is that the house is really clean. It is leaning a bit and the water damage on the walls, you know, but there aren't any bottles from bums or broken glass or dead bugs or anything. And the house is warm, not cold like it was outside. He goes back downstairs and finds the door to the basement, but it is locked, which he's glad because he doesn't want to go down there anyway. So he lays out his sleeping bag and gets in it and tries to fall asleep. It is totally dark in the house. After a while he hears a slam." The boy knocks on the wall behind him with his palm. "He sits up but he's not going to run. He'd been in the jungles of Vietnam and saw some terrible things. My friend told me. So he isn't scared of anything. He waits. Then the thump comes again, from the stairs. Coming down the stairs, slowly—" He continues to thump the wall. "Then he hears something in the basement, like a table getting thrown over. The thumps keep coming, out of time with each other. It is totally dark and he can hear the thumps coming closer, just around the corner from the room where he is crouched in the corner." His voice is barely a whisper now, everyone leaning forward nearly in a huddle, the smell of wintergreen gum blooming everywhere. "And the thumps stop and he can hear a sound, a wet sound like a fish's mouth and he picks up his flashlight that he brought back from the war and he turns it on and—" A pause. "There is nothing there. He gets up and walks out and hears a sound in the kitchen, where the basement door is. He walks in the little dot of light bouncing ahead of him. The basement door. He hears scratching on the other side of it. Louder and louder—" He was whispering. There was no other sound. "He reaches out. The knob is cold. He turns, pulls it open—"

From the stairwell, Leah and the girl hear a roar and cry. They startle, but do not run to see what happened. Leah is crying because the summer was over. They swore to call and write, but neither did and it was only years later that Leah thought to look the girl up on the Internet at work. At first she couldn't remember the girl's name. Leah sat blankly for several minutes, the syllables just out of tongue's reach. When it came to her, she spent nearly an hour tracking the girl down and finally found a blog she kept about her family. There were pictures of her five children in deeply saturated color. There were half-focused shots of the food they ate and requests for prayers for the little boy who had a problem with his lungs, his second hospitalization this year, and thanks for the gift cards to Target and Sears and Macy's, the boy had really scored this time, she joked. Even though the woman didn't mention it on her blog, Leah learned all about the woman's bankruptcy as well. There was a great deal to be learned and by the time that Leah left the office, late in the night, she heard someone outside in the dark, rooting through the office's trash cans.

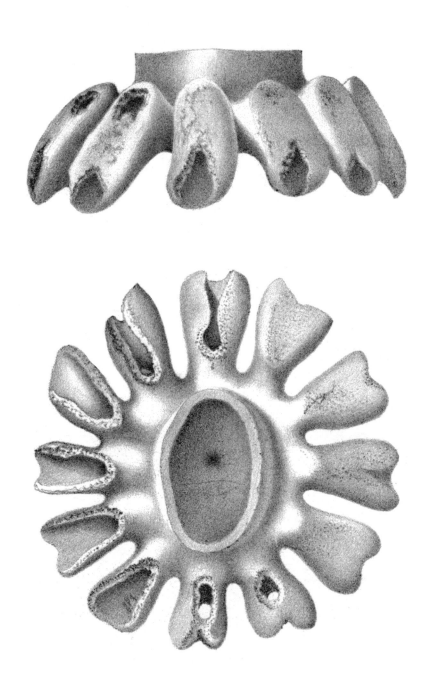

SUMMER AIR CHOKED WITH THE SMELL OF charcoal. Green grass growing wild in an unkempt backyard tickling and scratching young legs. The crash of drums from window-bound speakers, the increasing volume of the voices, the laughter at Rebecca Wilson's terrible jokes. Liquor spilled down knuckles as poorly made hamburger patties crackled on the grill. The speakers roared as the needle somewhere inside the house traced its narrowing gyre. Bees lobbed themselves at honeysuckle. Ants in chains along cracked cement walks. Daddy-long-legs invisible against gray bark and lichen and she closed her eyes, tipped her head back, baked her face in the sunlight and felt the blood in her head rush to the back of her skull. She told jokes, one after the other, increasingly filthy, dozens and dozens, increasingly bizarre, the stranger of her own construction. A young man, panting from running after a ball no one could keep their hands on, sat next to her in the grass, legs Indian style, and they talked. Barefoot. This friend of a friend or a cousin or other touched her wrist and her elbow and her shoulder, and his warm breath wafted over her warm face. And the sun set and the songs spun and the magnets moved air. "Stop me if you've heard this one before," she said. He didn't stop her. At some point, in the dark of the night, the music unable to obliterate the saw-bladed grasshoppers, Rebecca and this cousin of a friend of a friend rolled in the host's bed and then passed out on the back porch, curled up on artificial grass that covered cement.

And so on an afternoon two months later, Rebecca called

the host of the party and got the name of the friend with the cousin, embarrassed that she didn't even know his name and had to describe him three times before her friend could figure out whom she meant, and she called the cousin of the friend of the host and asked him to meet her for lunch. They met, hugged, he beamed and held the door open and told her that he was really happy to hear from her because he had a really nice time and she stopped him and said, "Listen, William, I need to tell you something," and he frowned, afraid, as though something unspeakably terrible were about to happen and Rebecca told him that she was pregnant. The young man silent for a second. He looked at her face and thought about how beautiful she was, how pale and wide her eyes were, how her hair fell in complex patterns around her ears and shoulders, about her long neck and the galaxy of freckles across her face and he said, "What do you want to do?" and she said she didn't know and the young man asked if she wanted to get married and Rebecca said, "I don't even know you. I didn't even remember your name." He looked hurt for a moment, fully realizing that she hadn't called him because she'd been thinking of him, unable to forget the fun they'd had that evening hanging out in the sun together. She'd only called him because they'd made a mistake. He sighed and said, "Whatever you want to do, I'll do it." She told him that she'd think about it and in the end, what could they do? They married in the summer of 1971 and she became Mrs. William Shepherd and they waited for the baby to come, but there was a problem and the thing was lost.

A year later, Rebecca lay in a room at the Ephraim McDowell Medical Center in downtown Crow Station, a brand new baby daughter that they named Leah. It was a Monday and the baby had come quickly, sluicing out like a wet potato out of wet hands, only thirty minutes after they arrived at the hospital. In the early days of Leah's life, when Rebecca thought about the child, she would think, 'it wriggled' or 'it is not making a sound' and then have to correct herself and think 'she wriggled' or 'she is not making a sound.' After so many months of thinking of the baby as some indeterminately gendered object that had set up residence in her uterus, it was difficult to think of the baby as a 'she.'

Rebecca kissed Leah's forehead. A bare dome still soft. She sniffed about the writhing red bean's features, trying to identify the unidentifiable baby smell, a smell that smelled the way terrycloth felt.

Neither Rebecca nor William Shepherd thought about the first pregnancy very often, until after Jacob disappeared. Though they never talked about it, that unnamed potential child would abruptly intrude upon their thoughts. Some nights, Rebecca would wake, certain she felt something inside of her move and she would start, worried about the baby, only to remember that she wasn't pregnant and that Jacob was gone.

A man called the nonprofit and asked the receptionist if she could answer some questions about Leah Shepherd. "I'm writing a newspaper article about her."

"They already did an article in the paper, didn't they?"

A pause and then, "I'm calling from the *Courier*. It is a special thing to celebrate her work, so if we could keep this a secret for now."

The receptionist loved secrets.

Who can see her crying? Who can feel the shuddering shoulders? The body shaking? Who can feel the damp cheeks, cool in the warm air, drying sticky like sweat? Light from windows.

The sound of rain. By the soft light of an open window, coffee cooling, rainbows swirling on the surface, cold.

The world choked with wolves ranging the neighborhood. With phantoms slipping from beneath bushes with long white hands to grasp young ankles. With men in coats with tape and box cutters. With pools of blood. With unheard screams. Some jowly pervert, eyes like empty sockets behind thick lenses, wagging himself at a passing school bus, ruining children. Homeless people even in a town like Crow Station, filthy things living out in the woods by the stream, slumping around town, reeking of human bodies, the knees of their ruined clothes betraying how they make ends meet. The world's mouth is open and it devours. The coffee cold and poured into the sink's black eye.

Her boy gone forever, her girl grown and she never calls, both emptied out to who knows where and Mrs. Shepherd says their names seven times in a row, quietly so as to not upset her husband, seeming to sleep nearby.

Lifting the receiver, she waited and then said, "Leah, honey, it's your mother."

What causes the bird to sing the night through? Mrs. Shepherd wondered. Spring rain flooded the basement and filled the house with the cold smell of new mold. *A brain disease?* she wonders. *A glaring of cats? A fit of avian insanity?* A glass horse held the basement door closed.

If daylight traffic noise is too great, it drowns the mating songs, forcing the birds to sing to one another at night, yet this bird sang alone. Just one voice outside of the open window, in the dark branches of a dark tree in the dark. If it is hoping to mate, it is out of luck. The windows had to be open because it is far too warm already to leave them closed, sealed up with the smell from the basement.

The one bird sang its one song and Mrs. Shepherd listened, certain that she was the one person awake in the neighborhood who could hear it. She rolled to find a comfortable spot between her husband and the wall.

Then one night, the singing was gone, but she was still awake, only now, listening to nothing. Distant cars. Voices. Dry leaves.

Once she watched the birds spiral in the swelling dusk, swirling above the houses and the street, above the galloping dogs and young people standing in a sulk on the darkening street corners, and then the birds, all with one movement and one mind, flew down into a chimney and disappeared and for a moment, she was delighted.

When Mr. Shepherd was a young boy, he ran naked through the streets with his best friend. Young bones strained at young skin, trying to grow right then and there. They'd painted each other with old house paint and screamed, "We're Indians. It's our war paint. We're at war." It didn't matter with what. They whooped and leapt. Cars careened to miss them as they darted along the blacktop. They swung sticks at dogs, sending the poor things spinning and howling.

Mr. Shepherd and his best friend ran home, cutting through backyards, painted bits bobbing, and when they got there, they found that water and soap did nothing to the now sick swirls of mustard brown that covered their thin chests and thin thighs. The housekeeper put them in a wash tub in the yard and poured gasoline over them. She scrubbed and scrubbed with something rough as the nude boys cried.

That evening, bouncing from twin bed to twin bed, Mr. Shepherd's best friend leapt too far, hit the wall with his nose and fell to the floor. Mr. Shepherd clutched the best friend and began to wail. "Dead, dead, dead!"

The Shepherd house was a plain house on a plain street that was once lined with oak trees, their broad branches arching over the pavement. Only a few still stood, the rest having fallen in one of the hundreds of thunderstorms that rolled through the town, and the few that still stood would themselves one day fall, cut by the power company to avoid an outage or touched by a bolt of lightening or simply told to bow by the voice of the wind.

Porch lights filled with dry brown bodies of innumerable winged insects and slowly bury the light.

In spring, Mrs. Shepherd swept windblown petals. She kept what was hers in order even as disorder crept in on all sides. She wanted it to be neat should her children come home. She called her daughter, left a message, swept windblown petals and thought to ask her husband to clean out the porch light when he got home. The porch light filled. The porch filled with people. Neighbors waiting, bringing food in pans and dishes. Waiting, saying things into the screen. Praying, our prayers, thoughts, thinking, our thoughts, help, we'll help, dear dear dear, prayer. Food to eat. The porch light dim on the dark porch. The light obscured by the fluttering.

He slipped into the house, having come from the apartment of one of the teachers he worked with, having told his wife that he just needed to go for a walk, having taken longer than he expected, having told the woman that they had to stop, because of his boy, that he needed to be home, that he couldn't do this, and the woman turned her face from him, understanding, having known, despite what she hoped, that this was the only way it ever could have ended, even before the boy was gone, the man having seeded this brooding worry over his family, and the woman, having felt him pulling away even as he protested that he would find a way to make their relationship work—his word—felt ashamed at the time to doubt him, to feel like he was already trying to get away from what he'd done, and now, hearing him tell her that he couldn't just leave his wife, she knew that she'd been right all along and suddenly felt how cheap her feelings had been, despite how unbearable they'd seemed at the time.

He left her apartment and slipped into his house and he let the door close, the faintest click and walked up the stairs as quietly as he could and longing to see his son asleep in his bed, to see the light from the hall fall across the boy's face, and upon pushing the door open, just barely open, his daughter began to scream and scream, a scream ripping air and boiling blood out of nothing and the lights in the room were on and his wife was up out of the bedroom, scared and he held the girl and tried to get her to be quiet.

When he finally got her back to bed, he followed his wife to their bedroom, she crawled into bed in the unbearable closeness of the dark and she curled up on her side of the bed, her curved spine toward him, seeking nothing from him, and he suddenly found that he needed her to wail and scream too, to try to crawl into his chest, but she didn't and he fell asleep on his back on his side of the bed and he drifted off, he at least felt happy that she was asleep. But she was wide awake, her eyes wide, her eyes wide open to the darkness and trembling and biting her lips in the gloom.

Leah Shepherd knew it was her fault that her brother was gone. At night she would lie in bed and pray to God for Jacob to come home. She prayed for her parents to never learn that it was her fault that he was gone. She was his big sister and she had failed to keep him safe. When in the bathroom she would take the hairbrush, a hard plastic thing that hurt when her mother drug it sharply through her hair, and she would slap her thighs with it until they glittered with pinpricks of pain, but it never seemed to cleanse her of the terrible feeling, the worm that hunted in her mind.

A week after Jacob disappeared, Leah went to her mother and said, "I saw a man looking at Jacob," and then, "I think that is who took him." Her mother began to cry and her father yelled at her for not telling earlier and she told them about the man in glasses she'd seen and her father called the police. Leah sat with the detective in the living room and looking down at her hands, tried to describe the man. He had glasses, she was sure. Maybe with wire frames. She didn't remember. His hair was brown or light brown or blond. He was tall, but stooped and looked small. His face was plain. He didn't have facial hair, but he hadn't shaved and she would see the stubble along the lines of his face. He was balding. Light had glistened on the bald places. He was white. Pale. But his face was red. She'd seen him behind the school. At the grocery store. Walking down the street. He'd looked at Jacob. He'd motioned to them once, but they'd run away. She remembered that for sure. Mr. Shepherd kept interrupting to remind Leah of things she'd said the first time that were different and after a few minutes, the detective was noncommittal.

A few months later, the Shepherds went to church for the first time since Jacob's disappearance. Mr. Shepherd was walking through the hallway after Sunday school and noticed the gentleman who taught one of the Sunday school classes, a balding man with thick glasses. Later, Mr. Shepherd couldn't really remember much other than seeing the man. He began to scream at the older man, accusing him, despite the fact that the man was nearly eighty and had been teaching his Sunday school class at the time of Jacob's disappearance, and when Mr. Shepherd hit the man in the face, the children who'd been standing in the classroom watching the argument began to scream and run through the church. "Murder, murder!" they screamed and the Shepherds had to attend a different church after that.

A suit was filed against Mr. Shepherd and Judge Whitehead, still then just Mr. Whitehead, represented him. He was able to, in light of the circumstances, get the charges against Mr. Shepherd dropped and the civil suit settled on terms that were pleasing to everyone. Judge Whitehead shook Mr. Shepherd's hand, smiled and said, "Anything you all need, just let me know." He didn't bill the Shepherds and always made good on his word to them.

Nighttime. The sound of thawing snow trickling through gutters. A newly purchased parcel of land in Bellevue Cemetery, the white seeping, but it would remain empty. Years had passed and Mr. Shepherd finally convinced his wife that it was necessary. For closure. But it would remain empty.

In bed, bedspread pulled up to their chins. They struggled to keep their collected warmth in the cold house. She had stopped crying. Eyes open, looking up at the black ceiling in the black room, watching the patterns of light cast by passing cars outside the bay window. Bands of white that shifted shape as they moved across the plaster.

This is how it was now, transmuted through some alchemical process into some new and degraded state. He wanted them to be over it and he felt a surge of anger at his wife's continued grief, then blushed with shame. His arm twitched. The dog was by the front door, sitting, waiting. It whined in periodic bursts. They did not hear their daughter moving about upstairs.

All night, cars passed, engines humming. Cars passed and passed. Her mother tried to imagine what the drivers of those cars must be feeling. Probably nothing. They probably never felt like this. Everyone was rushing home to be with their families.

Before her husband returned home, Mrs. Shepherd pulled the photo album from the shelf and singed herself on it. A yellow field full of cows, heads lowered and lowing, blue band above jaw of green trees. A drum to collect rainwater is dark from head lowered to it, lapping dark water, jittering face looking up. A long wall, dry masonry, separated the field from the neighborhood and morning broke over the green jaw and night rolled up for sleep over the town. The baby boy in the woman's arms pointing at trees and cows and trying to pat her hand on the surface of the water, cooing for more and more. The girl standing, gawking at lens.

She poured water into a clear plastic cup for her daughter. At night there is only the night and lagging in its midst a spill of stars, all of the stars that there ever were. Perhaps they do not have names. They are old waves that splash on her face and arms and legs. She bit her tongue after lashing at the girl. Bit till it bled.

The cows were gone, the field was empty, the tree had a disease of the bark. The fire went out. Then the garage door going up and she rushed, flushing to return the book to its place. For dinner: the rest of a box of penne and boneless chicken breast. There was nothing on television, but they watched nonetheless. "I like her voice."

From the road, the sky now sighing into violet through smudged window, across acres of yellow grass now shaded to indigo, whose contours are only the differences in their darkness, a small orange light outlasted.

Leah's mother's voice is always with her.

"Well, no. I mean, yes, there are lots of objects, obviously, more than we know, but also, you know, the universe is mostly empty space. But that's like all matter is mostly empty, you know, like we are made of molecules which are made of atoms which are made of electrons and protons and stuff which are made of subatomic particles like quarks and stuff and all that stuff, and atoms are mostly empty space around the electrons and protons and neutrons, but its all almost all empty space, you know. So when you think about it most stuff is empty and most of the universe is empty too just like that. So really there's mostly nothing in the universe because even that stuff that there is, is mostly nothing anyway."

Mr. Shepherd's parents' house was green, tucked in the back corner of the neighborhood. His father slept in the den, a dark wood-paneled room. Each morning he burned trash in the fireplace. Plastic, paper, and wood—the sick smell lingered all day. He smoked a pipe that filled the room with the sweet scent. There were shelves of mystery novels all throughout the house. The hardback dust jackets riddled with blood droplets and daggers. On one, the pale face of a young woman after her last exhalation. By Leah's grandfather's chair was an end table with an orange paperweight. Inside, the frozen body of a scorpion.

Unable to sleep, Leah got up and went to the window. A full moon and bright light seethed in the trees. Tree branches shattered moonlight. The neighbors' daughter pushed open a window and crawled out, crossed the yard. A black figure but white leopard spots scattered across her. She disappeared into the line of trees in the back of the yard on the far side. Figures moved there, waiting. She waited for her to come back, but fell asleep there on the floor, head against the sill. That is where her brother found her the next morning. The sun was high and the house was full of the scent of bacon spitting in a skillet.

When Mrs. Shepherd visited her old college roommate, Leah had to sit on the back porch. In the living room where the women sat and drank tea and talked, there hung the stuffed head of a deer. Antlers reaching wide. Black eyes dulled by dust. Her mother talked to her old roommate about the old roommate's divorce. "Bless," her mother would say. She sipped sweet tea.

Leah sat on the back porch and waited, bored. It was summer. She scratched her bare legs and talked to herself. From behind the hedge, she saw two girls in white, peeking. She tried not to look directly at them, ashamed of her curiosity.

Later, at home in bed, she could hear the neighborhood children outside in the summer evening, screaming to one another. She never saw the two girls peeking around the hedge again, though maybe their voices were a part of the throng outside.

She told Jacob, "God created the world out of nothing: There was only God before. All there was was God and he made a void in himself large enough for the world. God wanted there to be something that was not-God. The ocean made the shore just so it could lap."

Mrs. Shepherd looked into her daughter's room and asked, "Who are you talking to?" Leah shrugged.

They feel warmth radiating. He stops, turns to her, about to speak for a moment the old rush, the old feeling passes through her, a swelling wave, just like when they first met, first dated, were first married, first learned each other's bodies. He looks into her eyes in the dim light of the distant streetlamp. Faces mostly in shadow. She feels this for a moment, a flicker, and then it is gone and she feels nothing. And then, warm hum gone, more gone than she'd ever felt before. Only a hollow, a bell between hours, denuded of vibration.

Her face shows none of this as they stand there. He is unaware. His face is flushed and he leans in to kiss her and she puts her hand on his shoulder and lets him.

At home, they undress and slip into bed. He wriggles in the dark up against her body, whispers something blurry and drifts off. She stays awake for a long time after, but how long, she has no idea. The memory of her children, her girl and her boy, crowd back, and she is ashamed to have failed to keep them foremost in her mind, if even for an evening. This is all there will ever be. Her years learning to wriggle and learning to walk and her degrees and her promotions and summers at the beach and the children new in her arms. This is all that will ever be.

Rebecca Wilson slept with her sisters in the tall grass as their father shot at the stars and called out names at the tall trees closing around him. She remembered her sisters and she told William about sleeping in tall grass under a sky pregnant with little fires and how their father would wail and wail, how he would finally fall silent and stand in the door, a sliver of night fallen and snoring in the light of the kitchen. William put his arms around her to comfort her, but she pulled away. It was a long time before he learned that she did not like being touched when she was upset. After the children were born, something changed in Rebecca's father and he stopped drinking. He lived alone on his farm and made an effort to get close to the one daughter that still lived in the state.

Rebecca Shepherd remembered the gauze of scum on the surface of a lake and called her father on his birthday and brought the children to see him and they watched as Leah and Jacob ran around the yard of the farmhouse.

Her sisters, gone to Florida as a teen in trouble, or married to a preacher, or drowsing by a pool.

In college, Leah went on a date with a man who claimed to be a jockey. They sat in the cab of his pickup truck after a drive-in movie and he talked about his ex-wife, spittle flying off of his lips onto the steering wheel. He talked about how Mexicans were riding all the good horses now. He fell silent for long stretches. Afterward, he pawed and panted and she held him at bay with one long arm. When she would not relent, he kicked her out of the cab and drove off, leaving her alone on a rural road. Deep green trees in the deep night are darker than anything else, especially as high-summer air rambles through.

As she walked, she tried not to think about the encyclopedia entry on Legal Issues Related to the Disposal of Dead Bodies that she'd read:

—failure to bury or dispose of bodies; burial without a permit; wrongful disposal of the body; delivery of dead bodies to the loved ones; to kin; for dissection; for ridicule; for viewing; for rueful viewing; for nothing; civil liability for mutilations, generally; a record of disinterment—

So many things can go wrong, even after you are done. When she returned to campus, her roommate was still awake, waiting in the semi-dark. "Sooooooo?"

Her stomach covered in ticks. They'd followed tree trunks painted red and wound up hills in cool shade. Shadows slanted down and the path rose. They heard people walking in the water but couldn't see them, heard dogs fluttering above. They'd brought books to read, but they were left open, pages to the ground, unread, as the young couple pressed into one another, pulled up shirts and unbuttoned and unzipped and the scratches of grass and rocks on skin and the warm sigh of summer on their faces and thighs and stomachs. The saw and chip of summer. She asked him to pull them off and his face twisted in disgust. The swell of cicadas, some lost Blue Ridge Brood. Leah Shepherd sighed and pulled them off herself with a match. She drug her shirt back down.

The engagement would not last. He told his family that she was cold and that the doctorate meant more to her than he did, that she didn't support his career, that she was hell-bent on moving back to Kentucky—Dear God—and in the end he hadn't even been that attracted to her physically but was yet another example of him feeling sorry for a girl, being there for her as a friend and supporting her, and mistaking that feeling of duty for love or something. In retrospect, he felt more embarrassed than anything else. He told his family that he wasn't angry with her for the two years they were together, the time he spent on her, the time he could have given to his research. Yes, if he'd spent that time on his work, he probably could have found something better than these adjunct positions, he'd had promise, all his teachers had told him about his promise, but he did not blame her for the years she took. Rather, he felt like the experience might have left him with material for a novel.

Plus, don't you know, she didn't even finish her dissertation, leaving with a masters and not much more. Leah didn't explain the failure of the engagement to her parents because they didn't ask.

Derrick Green would sit next to Leah in every class and ask her if she wanted to get coffee and she agreed. He was light-hearted and kind and when she didn't care to talk, he respected her. When he told the joke that had ended it all, Leah hadn't exploded in tears or rage or fists, which she would have been entitled to, but she receded, just far enough that he understood that he could no longer reach her. If only he'd known, he would never have told such a joke, at least not in front of her, but he never knew because she never explained, never told him anything about her childhood other than it wasn't worth talking about. In that, he felt that she bore much of the blame.

At a party, standing with some of the other young men in the program, he told the joke and they laughed, all but her. The same laugh he always got, a pause, a moment of uncertainty, and then the burst of rough laughter, involuntary, and then a second cascade of laughter, laughter of embarrassment at having laughed at such a joke. She walked off and he could immediately tell that he should not have told it, beyond the usual disgusted smirk he would occasionally get, usually from women.

And that car, he thought, *that car that took up more money to maintain than it was worth. What a wasteful woman, throwing money at that blue monstrosity just because she thinks it makes her look cool.* Derrick would plead with her to trade it in and get something more reliable—he couldn't come get her every other week when her car decided to give out while she was out on a Sunday drive. They faded and fell apart and the absence of any real distress that he could understand angered him. He felt like he deserved something more direct from her for the crumbling relationship, but Leah would only say, "There's nothing wrong. I promise." Or "There is nothing wrong except you keep asking me what is wrong." Or "What do you want from me?" And he began to pick fights just to get a response, but nothing worked. Leah was a rowboat in a lake cut loose from the dock, slowly drifting out into the haze of morning, fading, blank and white and then one day gone.

He told his parents and they asked him to pray, and the family bowed their heads and prayed that the woman who'd so wounded their son would open her heart to a man someday and learn the peace that can be found in being led. At dinner, he told his father, "Oh, you have to hear this joke."

"I want to show you something strange."

The variety of shades of gray outside her window shifted their hue and quality and she opened another file to begin working. As she jotted notes in the margin of an application for aid, her mind wandered. *How much of what I've known in my life, have I forgotten?*

She remembered the nights when she would hear the door downstairs open, the faint click of the doorknob turning, the squeal of hinges, something coming, steps in the hall, steps on the stairs, and then a pause, just outside of the room she shared with her brother, and remembering this, it all felt to her as though it could never have been any other way. God, whisper everything away, she prayed, away from us, and perhaps God heard because eventually the steps moved on down the hallway, slow steps fading into the settled silence of the dark house and the children would, despite the red feeling in their throats, do the thing they never thought they would do again—fall asleep.

She remembered the nights telling Jacob how, if he didn't stop talking to her and let her sleep, that a creature would come for him and she remembered the glee she felt when she heard him cry and the shame she felt when she heard him cry, and the feeling now, in her bed in her apartment, thinking back to the boy in his bed that she terrified and she felt herself cave in. But she was just a child too, she told herself, and then remembered the sound, in the nights after he was gone, the sound of the door opening in the well of night, the sound of someone, or something moving in the house, and the sudden fear that her stories had come true. She never once considered that it might be Jacob coming home and only now, kicking her blanket off of her legs in the warm bedroom, despite the open window, did she realize that she never once considered it. He was always final.

Her palms and fingers were pink. Her fingernails black crescents. Broken rock's jutting chins swaddled in lichens and small plants. Pale yellow, yellow-green, green-brown. Roots knobbed and gnarled. Dipped and rose, rocks and mud. Dead leaves—red and orange. The nothing made a sound. Nothing scurried about at the slap of her soft shoes. The trees crowded out the dimming rays of the white sun. She walked by the stream. She walked past the last turn of the stream, and kept walking, beyond where there was a path. Something red fluttered in the distance.

Leah saw a table. It was round and covered in a bright blue cloth.

The quaking of spring wriggling out of winter clouds black draped cracks of purple light quivering up from the ground power-out houses dead in the eyes and after the trembling stopped she drove through her neighborhood in her blue car to see uprooted trees and tatters of green leaves littered across wet pavement a dead crow and she killed the headlights for a moment and was in complete darkness.

The next night she stayed up until dawn but nothing happened worth staying up for, a new sun born above backlit firs but it was a faraway thing.

The light that comes through high windows is different than any other kind of light and it reaches through an empty room.

The hunter green Jeep was nearly black parked at the edge of the gravel. It was deep night and below the bending branches of the bare trees, the starless sky was meaningless and void, in her blue car, Leah cruising slowly along the country road, following bending fences and falling rock walls. It had passed into being Sunday at some point. The clock in the dashboard suggested an hour that was wrong and had been wrong for years.

She coughed, took a sip of the soda she held between her legs and felt a sudden caul of exhaustion. She passed the spot with the Jeep twice, parked at the edge of the woods. A small, soft night.

In her blue Bug, Leah Shepherd circumnavigated Crow Station at night. Cassette in cassette deck, she pulled from the parking lot of the apartment complex out onto the empty street. An empty world. Streets lit by streetlamps, perfect puddles of pink light periodic in the still darkness of an autumn night. And then the church and the gate to the cemetery and the college and the viaduct and the train tracks and the Christian Children's Home and the county school and then the bypass. She sat at a red light, bathed in red light, listening to the engine idle and the cassette rewind. When she was at home, when she was at work, even in her memories, she was what she'd always been, this daughter, this sister, this woman. Only in her car in the blank hours, in the empty streets of the dark county, could she be some other thing. Or nothing. This humming barrow, shrouded in the endless looping of the cassette tapes of her favorite songs, popular songs purchased from mail-order companies.

She turned off of the bypass and took a route along a twisting road into the heart of the county. In the dark, her headlights illuminated the fences of pastures and they flickered by in the corner of her eyes. The world that existed was only the two protrusions of light along the gray blacktop. She passed obscure pull-offs, gravel spots by bushes or down by the lake. Sometimes there were cars parked in these places, teenage couples seeking refuge from prying eyes of over-protective parents. Sometimes, two or three cars, parked with plenty of space between, the only lights those that glimmer from inside the obscured windows. Sometimes a car is parked and she could see someone standing alone in the dark, leaning against the black trunk of a black tree, the only light, a carbuncle smoldering at face-level and a hand disappearing into the dark. How did she look to this person? Was she just another figure in the dark? Another sliver of shadow? And then by some magic, her winding and weaving would lead her back again to the bright edge of Crow Station. Its pink reflection against the sky, the inside of an eyelid.

Leah pulled into the parking lot of a gas station and fished enough change from the console to purchase a bottle of water. As she came out, she noticed an orange car pull in. Leah slipped into her seat, but didn't start the car. She watched a young woman park at a pump, fill the gas tank, standing still as the pump's meter flew and then walk in, slowly, through the brightness, into the even brighter of the small market, to pay, face indistinct in the light, hair short, small hoop earrings glinting. Watching this woman, Leah sipped cold sips that made her teeth ache. Her still warm car *tick tick tick*ed as it cooled in the cold air. The young woman came out, got in her car, and drove off. Leah followed.

Through the middle of town, heading north. The lights were green. The streetlamps vanished ahead of the orange car in one point, some distant end of town. Past the churches and grocery stores on the north end of town and the country club and over the old blue bridge that crossed the lake, into the dark of the county again. She kept her distance. It wasn't difficult to follow. There wasn't anyone else on the road. Leah sang along with the cassette. The road wound and there was no light other than the headlights of the cars. She would lose it around a corner, but on a straight away see its distant red signature. Where the trees did not overhang the road, the moon granted the void around her some depth.

The orange car turned right onto a thin gravel drive. The trees were close and indistinct. Leah turned off her headlamps. She could see the taillights ahead and the partial moon distinguished gravel and grass. The orange car stopped in front of a small house, a small yard cut from the thick woods around it. She stopped her car at the same time, back in the trees, in the deep shadow, but with the house and orange car in full view. The car's headlights set the small front porch of a ranch house with white vinyl siding aglow. The front door of the house opened and a man came out. Middle aged, perhaps late thirties. It was dark and the bright headlights against his face washed out his features, so it was impossible to tell what he looked like beyond the fact that he had short hair, a T-shirt and jeans on. The car's lights went off and the young woman got out. She trotted up to the steps and he stepped down. They embraced, kissed. She handed him a plastic bag and he held the door open for her.

The night was blue. The sky and air and trees and gravel were all blue black. The only other color was the one window of the house that was on—the warm light inside was yellow. From the car, she could see into a small living room. Watched them cross the room, speaking to each other. The cassette flipped sides. They were gone for a few moments, in the kitchen putting whatever was in the bag away. Then they were back. They held each other again and stood there, her head coming to his chin. As she watched them, she could still not see the young woman's face. Even when she was turned toward the window, it was too indistinct. She wore a blue University of Kentucky sweatshirt that was baggy but she could see the outline of her breasts underneath. She wore dark jeans. She stretched her legs and feet to reach the man to kiss him again. He had thick legs and waist—probably a former high school football player. Probably didn't get a scholarship to go to one of the big schools. Took some classes at the community college and helps his father out with his painting business. The young man was handsome—his hair tousled and his face open and pleasant. He already had lines around his face from smiling. They just stood there in their living room, holding each other, not speaking or moving, not even swaying. Still. And she watched until with a staccato kiss they released and walked out of view. Leah flushed, thinking about how this young couple would never have access to this part of their life, to Leah watching them kiss. In some far off year, when they were old and reminiscing, they would remember those young days when they lived out in the country, in the woods, in that little house and how they would kiss and hold one another and strip each other naked and roll around free from everything, and they would never know that along the edge of these memories Leah sat, just out of view, her face bathed in the little light that came from the dashboard.

She sat there several minutes longer, staring into the unchanging empty room, then started the car and backed up a little ways and then when the house was out of view and she was on the road, her headlights on again, filled with a violent loneliness that the moon did not understand.

A darkening silo. A rolling spill. A rolling split of hill. Of lengthening day-sore gray. Her weight on her forearms and for a moment the perfect construction: The shiver of stars as the legs disappear through the surface. Obliteration of a dual sky brought low for even them to play in. She couldn't much see her, just the sliver of pale like a white comma on a black page. She waited. They would cast into each other. Gaudy sky of a late afternoon. Black moons darned underneath her nails. The last light glinting the dome of the streetlight and would have reached her face and body, lit the very few stray strands of hair and shivered her body with luminescence and delicacy had she not been in the wrong place for this to happen.

Calm outside, no stars, streetlights lit pools in darkness, wet sidewalk shimmering. A few months later—

In the bathroom the warm steam from the hot water taps slowly seeping out of the cracked window. The last bell rang. Light, pale, fell in and lit everything evenly, even deep in the crevices and valleys of her heavy clothing.

She watched her children shrink to black sparks, trailing way through the gray streets and gleaming muddy fields and yards.

The short clack of echo rocketed in her ear, high and grinding.

Though having sprung off in different directions they meet again at the place in space where the universe loops around again and meets itself. There they connect, intertwine and forget which was which.

A tree and its roots.

The Commonwealth of Kentucky was once an ocean. Not a land of bluegrass but an endless expanse of blue waves, waters full of indescribably creepy creatures that frisked and scuttled below the surface of a sea that was ancient even then, but over time the waters receded and the dead of those obscure monstrosities slumbering on the floor were battered and crushed by currents to grains and granules. Trilobites, brachiopods, gastropods, crinoids, edrioasteroids. Crushed and crushed and crushed. The bodies sifted down, each upon each, and as ages passed they became stone, the strata of which tell and retell a story. Limestone, the living rock, the soft monument, rainwater washing it away in drips and drabs, year after year, leaving a vast vein of caves. At every moment that soft rock erodes away under unsuspecting feet.

The City of Crow Station is in the exact geographic center of the state, more or less, and as a result is directly over the center of the yawning void. Bats and blind shrimp and the bones of lost children. One day it is going to collapse, the entire Commonwealth of Kentucky, every bronze statue of a thoroughbred, every distillery and secret crop hidden between the rows of corn. The City of Crow Station, home of the first Post Office west of the Allegheny Mountains and the first ovariotomy. Harrod County and its vast fields of cud-chewing bovines. The Bluegrass and the Pennyroyal and the Jackson Purchase. Those last limestone pillars that hold the whole Commonwealth aloft will give way and the schools and real estate agencies and farm supply stores and hogs and horses and ducks will tumble down into that bleak blackness. Children will tumble and poor farmers whose breath is scented with family recipe mash and estate lawyers still in reverie of the fees for the administration of a dead millionaire and beautiful long-legged high school boys and strong-armed girls will tumble. Body over body, legs twirling, endlessly down and down, passing the slower bodies of former loves and the caskets of old teachers spilling open.

This ancient abyss waiting the sun's call to rise. The lifeless swells of sand waiting the air's call to bloom and glow. The worn away bones of every scuttling and nameless thing waiting to rise as rock and mountain.

"LEAH?" SHE LOOKED UP AT THE MAN STANDING next to her table. Behind him were banks of windows looking out on the midday light of Crow Station, Kentucky. He was tall and middle aged. "Yes?"

"Leah," he said again. "Can I sit?" She nodded. She had just taken a sip of her sweet tea and her lips felt wet. The man sat and looked at her, smiling, without saying anything. "What can I do for you—I'm sorry I didn't catch your name." The man was smiling at her and not saying anything and she became very uncomfortable and was about to say something when he began again. "I guess I shouldn't be surprised. It's been so long and I can't say that I would have recognized you had I not seen the article. Leah, it's me. Jacob."

Broken men and women, slight shuffling and trembling before the weight of the hollow light. Why the whispers? they wonder. Each shuffles, each sweeps their shattered fragments along the halls or through rain water wet streets. Under light, under light: fluorescent and green—a child once cut a paper to seam a scene—a boy chased from the arcade, from the lush hill by a man of some shadowy bulk—or knelt in the floor by the window at night, chin on sill, eyes crossing, stemming the tide of sleep no more, thinking: nothing. At night their beds are rafts on a wide river or man-made lake. Their stuffed dogs and blankets:

travelers met at the last station, ragged and hungry. The hot stream that flows backward when they hear the slow songs crackle on the radio, is never going to empty into a sea. They will realize as they brush the little bit of hair back from their glassed eye, filling out the same form for the nth time. They will think, "——." They can only think of the book they read once. They will remember one day while passing a used bookstore, seeing a copy in the window: rain rotted, binding blown, mold mournfully draped like crepe. They will remember the book they read each night for a week straight, under the covers, lamp light or by the glow of the radio. Two children, siblings, the bag of jewels or cash, the rich married couple, the unlocked doors, a man in a black coat under trees by the beach, backlit by the plump moon: the moon knows nothing about any of this. Then they will walk on, will not remember how the book ends. Then they will go back to work.

When she thought about it later, she could not remember what her feeling had been. Had she wanted to embrace him? Had she wanted to scream and run? Had she been afraid? Had she felt a swell of recognition and love? When she thought about it later, she couldn't remember having any reaction. She could clearly remember everything about the moment—the man, the windows bright behind him, the smells and sounds of the small restaurant at lunch time. She could even see herself, as though she'd not been part of the scene, only observing it from afar. Every mote lolling on a slight breeze of greasy air. The clack of every tooth of every person around them on bent tines. The swirling scents of stale coffee and ancient grease deep-frying the town into oblivion. The arc of a fly battering its black body in a corner. In that moment, Leah Shepherd was aware of every contour of the physical universe which she was the center of with this man sitting across from her in front of the windows bright with the day's light, but what she felt inside was a complete mystery to her. She was a surface across which creation played, but below, no light prevailed. She'd sat and she'd listened to him.

The man told her his story: His name was John Rhodes and he'd grown up in Florala, Alabama, the sole son of a single father. They'd lived in a small cinder block house out on a state highway. This father had worked in construction and taken odd jobs on weekends and evenings to make ends meet. To make sure there was food on the table and clothes on the boy's back. A good man, one who would pick up a hitchhiker no matter how filthy she was. John remembered that the man had taken his work boots and taped them up rather than buy new ones so that John could have new clothes for school. He said he couldn't remember much from his early life. Some images, disconnected from one another. Not even images, but shards of feelings, something deep and hidden. It wasn't something that had ever bothered him. No one remembers everything about their early years—he just couldn't remember more than most. His father had tried to give him everything and John had worked hard, though he'd only done average in school and he'd grown up and graduated high school and started working in construction like his father.

Had he said *father*? Or *daddy*? *Pa*? Father felt wrong, but that's what she remembered. Had he called him *the old man*?

A few months ago, his father had passed away and when John was going through the old man's belongings, he'd found several articles from Kentucky newspapers about a boy that had gone missing. At first, John hadn't thought anything of it, other than being interested in the story. After finding the tenth or so story he began to wonder about his father's interest. That night, when he was lying in bed, in his father's bed actually, having taken the larger room for himself, John began to think about his own childhood and the story of the missing boy and it was like when you hear a song and can almost remember what its name is and with a quake you remember and it just falls into place. Before that moment, for the whole of his years, John said he'd felt like his life had been flat, like it existed only in two dimensions, like he was a drawing, but that was all he'd known so he hadn't realized that there was any other way to exist, but once he recognized that melody, his life had lifted up into a new realm. He couldn't sleep and his skin capered with electricity.

When he was growing up, his father never talked about John's mother. The old man said that she'd died when John had been a young baby, and John never bothered his father about it because it was clearly painful to him and the old man just wasn't the type of man who talked about such things, even though he didn't even know what his mother's name was or what she looked like. He couldn't remember her at all and there weren't any pictures in the house. Yet, as he cleaned out the old man's ranch house, John found nothing about his mother. Maybe his father had gotten rid of it all after she died in some explosion of grief, but the man had receipts and notes and cancelled checks going back decades, so it didn't seem likely that he would have been able to remove all trace of his deceased wife from the house. Not only were there no pictures of her, there were no pictures of anyone at all. There weren't even any pictures of John from when he was very young. He found a letter from a landlord in Crow Station, Kentucky, returning a deposit on an apartment and some pay stubs from a warehouse there as well. His father had never talked about living in Kentucky and as far as the man knew, he and his father had always lived in Alabama. John couldn't find anything from before he was seven years old in the house.

His whole life until two weeks ago, he'd thought of himself as John Rhodes, but now, in the span of a few short days, he'd not only lost his father, but he'd lost himself. He tried to imagine his father as a kidnapper and it seemed outrageous to him. While the man had been emotionally aloof and stern, he'd been a good father. The man had broken himself working to provide for John and John felt guilt thinking such terrible things about him. Yet the evidence was, if not irrefutable, painfully intriguing. So he decided to take some time off work and come up to Kentucky to see if he could prove to himself who he was, one way or the other.

He'd been in Crow Station for three days, trying to find more information before he showed up on the Shepherd doorstep and announced himself as the long lost son. One of the first things he'd done was to go to the town cemetery and look for his grave. One of the last articles that his father had was a short piece about how the Shepherd family had finally had Jacob Shepherd declared legally dead. John walked around the cemetery in the growing dusk, looking at the marble and granite, the names and years, the elderly and the infant. He'd looked for Jacob's grave, hoping that if he saw it, there would be some shock of recognition if he was indeed, Jacob Shepherd. As he walked it got darker and darker and he became more and more desperate to find the grave. He heard some voices and looked across the cemetery and saw a group of children running around and hollering at each other, laughing and screeching like children just on the cusp of growing up do, unable to keep anything in, and he watched them and thought about how he'd never had that life. He'd never been young. He'd never been a child. He'd only ever worked and slept. A terrible desire to run at the children swelled in him, to begin to scream and yell, to shout at them—for what? For enjoying themselves? For being disrespectful in the graveyard? He didn't know and he didn't do anything but stand in the path of the evening's shadows. Out there among those stones that the children wound through was one that had his real name on it, he knew it, a marker not for a dead child but for a lost life and in that instant, he knew for sure. He left without ever finding his own stone.

He didn't want to cause anyone any unnecessary pain if he could help it, but he had to claim his life. The next morning, as though God had finally given up on the joke, John saw her photograph in the newspaper, where she'd won her award for service, and seeing her, he knew she was his sister and he had to see her first. He'd been trying to get hold of her at her office for a few days, but was happy that he hadn't been able to because he wasn't sure what he would have said on the telephone.

Leah listened. The restaurant around them had disappeared. She looked at the man sitting across from her. Did he look like her father? She couldn't tell if he did or if it was the power of suggestion. The waiter came and refilled her sweet tea and John Rhodes ordered a coffee. "You don't mind, do you?" he asked, but the waiter was already gone, so it didn't matter what Leah thought. "No," she said.

"Thanks, I didn't—"

"No, I mean, you aren't him. You aren't Jacob." Her voice was shaking. She rose, drawing some bills from her purse, and tossing them on the table, began to walk out. He leapt up and followed her. "Leah, hold on. Leah," he said, but she didn't stop. He grabbed her arm. It was dull and weightless, like a change in air pressure. She was at her car in the parking lot and he ran up behind her, grabbed her shoulder, "Listen, don't run away from me. I know how this sounds—"

"This is bullshit," Leah said, her voice flat. "My brother is dead. He's been dead for a very long time. You can't do this to me and you can't do this to my family."

The man's face flashed and he pushed himself between her and the car but said nothing. She watched his lips writhe, seeking

something there and then pushed him aside, got in her car and
drove off.

When she thought about it later, Leah tried to remember his
face but couldn't, instead only able to conjure something from
family photographs that adorned her parents' den. She'd wanted
to always remember, but the objects kept to serve as shrines
quickly crowded everything out. Silver platters of food clanging
loudly on the hardwood floor. Laughter. Great links of meat.
Great quantities of cold clear liquor flowed briskly. Her mother
in the next room singing hymns. She woke in her bed in her
one-bedroom apartment. She woke still hearing the singing. The
organ's staccato jabs and a bass's bubbly bursts. The heat kicks
on. Wool is quiet. The window wasn't open. Had Jacob been
living somewhere all of those nights of her mother's bloodless
keening? Had he been living somewhere all of those mornings
when her father stood at the window and didn't speak? Had he
been living somewhere while they fed on nothing but his death?
Black milk in pools on dark ground. She fell asleep on her futon
and did not dream.

The window is all dog-eared salty stains. Rainwater slips
down and patters on gradually looser wires, vibrating slower,
each identical movement pulled further apart until it echoes long
after the faces have dropped and shimmered away. Then it is day
again.

A bird got in and fluttered about the drop ceiling, singing its
panic. An old man bought hot dog buns and iodine. A woman
bought strawberry glaze and tonic water. Children bought comics and tubes of flavored sugar. The bird dove at bald heads in

produce as the produce manager swung a filthy mop in the air, defending perfectly piled bell peppers. Over one hundred dollars worth of meat was stolen by a woman in a pink overcoat. A man with troubled teeth cashed checks and did a dance. In the back, a pallet of milk overturned and a white sea spread. The bird swelled into shadows.

Three days later, Leah Shepherd woke to the claxon of her cell phone. Her mother was in tears, unable to talk. Leah listened, tried to soothe her, but knew, knew before she even told Leah.

Today in the mail there had been an envelope, no return address, Crow Station post mark. An old article about Jacob and nothing else.

"Who would do such a thing?" Mrs. Shepherd asked, crying into the telephone. Leah tried to comfort her mother, and it worked for a time, but the next day, the Shepherds received a second envelope.

She told him that he had to stop, talking on her work telephone in her office late at night, not wanting this man to have her cell phone number.

"Stop what?"

"You know what." Nothing. He was making her say it. "The envelopes."

He told her not to talk to him like that. He told her that he'd done nothing. He kept saying *Nothing, nothing.* Had he even asked her for anything? *Nothing.* She responded with silence. Had he? *Nothing.* He huffed like an impudent heir. Her throat searing with blood. He told her that he was going to see them, her parents.

She offered him money, what money she had, to stay away.

"That's not what I want," he said, but she knew he was lying and she waited for him to prove her right, for the sharp inhalation of breath and for the studied reluctance, for the voice that sounded like swooning shadows cast by swinging lanterns, but the man was silent and between them hunkered nothing but the hiss of the line and from it emerged the finest crazing on the surface of her certainty. The lights were out in her office and Leah felt that she was alone in a vast, empty space and that the only other thing in existence was this man's voice, but even that was now gone, leaving nothing but soft breathing that she could barely hear, somewhere else in Crow Station. Cars passed outside of her office, casting their shapes as they no doubt passed outside of wherever he was. And there was then a moment when she almost believed that she was wrong.

But when John Rhodes began to speak again, he said, "All right. Fine. I thought—" a long pause and sounds she could not identify, "—I didn't think this is how this would end up. When I thought about it. I saw different things. I don't know who you think I am or what I done, but—" and again he paused for a long time before saying, "I been without you all and I can do without you all." They agreed to meet the next night at the grocery store on the bypass. He'd stop there on his way out of town and she would give him what she had and he would leave before the snow storm that they were calling for trapped him.

Leah sat in her office, the only light from the power switch on her computer, listening to the dark outside, hoping that whatever was lurking there was gone.

The snow came from nowhere, falling softly on a Sunday night across Crow Station, Kentucky, covering the swelling hills and limestone teeth that jutted up from yellow-green jaws, and everyone stopped to watch it come down, glittering flames in the long light of the setting sun. At a red light Leah Shepherd leaned over and pressed her nose to the window and looked up into the pink sky at the pink snow that sifted slowly from pink clouds that floated above her. The radio scanned the stations trying to find the perfect song for the moment, but she found only the soft pleas of commercials, so she shut it off. Silence flickering, bright snow in headlights passing, she thought about her brother and could still hear his voice calling her name, *Leah! Leeeah!* again and again, his voice piling in drifts around her legs and hips and chest. The light changed.

At the grocery store, she waited for John Rhodes like he asked, milling among the crowds of people, all hollering at one another, all jawing on cell phones, all panting and cursing. She checked the time. The grocery store was the last thing on the way out of town, the upper edge of Crow Station, the last light before you emptied out on those long country roads and wound yourself through hills dotted with dead trees, bent black branches, howling in the hard wind. The grocery store had seen better days. Its tile floor was pocked and scarred, the ceiling tiles bulging inward from ancient leaks and the flickering fluorescent lights made everything inside look cheap and stale. Usually the grocery store was empty, its shoppers having tapered off in the years, but that night, as the snow came, it was full and the man was late. Leah checked her cell phone. Up and down the aisles, looking at everything on the emptying shelves, looking at the women and men and children, listening to their voices, voices that intermingled with the voices she heard every day, with the voices of the women and their children, the howling men outside the windows of the shelter, the boys on bikes harrowing the dead-end streets looking for lights to break, the voices of her mother and father in their room, whispering, thinking Leah was asleep and could not hear them, with Jacob's voice that she heard walking in the wind outside of her window, and Leah traced the creases at the corners of their mouths and the shadows under their eyes, the swaying backs and slung forward guts and the skin taut over tired skulls and she could hear all of them all at once, but the man who said he was her brother was not there. Old men smiling at old women and children with cherubic cheeks pitching fits on the dirty tile floors and all around them the trembling motet of people certain they are about to die, voices in close cacophony moving in waves, the voices she heard every day as she listened to the white noise for her brother's voice, her real brother's voice to rise through the confusion and speak to her but all she heard was *Leah! Leeeaah! Help!* because that was all that was left of his voice.

After an hour of waiting, Leah called him again. She could not think of him as Jacob because she knew that he wasn't. He was just an awful man from Alabama who'd seen her in the newspaper and decided her family would be an easy mark. He was right, she thought. No one answered. She walked to the front of the store and looked out. The fat flakes were making their way down through the still rays of the security lights in the parking lot and it was beginning to coat the ground and was swirling like snakes on the road. She waited a little while longer, feeling the envelope in her pocket. She waited and it grew late. She held her hips at an angle, a swell of quills below her skin. Everyone talking, everyone singing, every throat raised in song, every voice distinct and chiming in harmonies not yet understood by human ears, standing as though they'd always been standing in that exact place, always would be standing there, waiting. She slept and sleep was waiting. She woke and waking was waiting. She worked and work was waiting. She walked by the stream in the trees and walking was waiting. She listened to the voice in the wind that moved through the trees and the voice was waiting until she was ready to speak. If the man came, she knew what she would say to him. She knew that as she handed him the envelope that she would tell him what she'd never told anyone—not her parents or her one friend in high school or any of the men she'd dated or any of the people she'd worked with. She'd tell him about how each night she listened for Jacob's voice, his voice. How she would lie in bed and listen for him somewhere in the darkness inside and how during the day as she listened to the women at work or to a couple at a table nearby during lunch, she listened for Jacob's voice. How she wanted to hear it again so as to erase the voice of his that was there, constantly in her mind, his young voice calling out to her, screaming her name and begging for help and how she'd sat inside and ignored it, mad at him for getting her in trouble the day before. She'd thought he'd been putting on so that she would run to him, like she always did, and would beg him to come home, so she sat in the living room as her parents busied themselves upstairs getting ready for church, and Leah ignored his pleas. And that was the last time she heard his voice. She would tell John Rhodes this, this secret thing she'd never even articulated to herself, and she would ask him, no matter who he was, to forgive her.

The music was barely audible over the babble. Everything that exists now has always existed in one shape or another: This line of people, this snow falling, this light from flickering bulbs overhead. All have always been and would always be, forever and ever, no matter what Leah hoped. The throng around her closed in and no one moved and she felt too warm and too close and too tired and could see the glitter of the snow outside, but she felt calm. *He isn't Jacob*, she thought, *Jacob is gone*, and she felt as though her chest was so heavy that she was being pulled to the floor, to the center of the Earth, but even as she thought this, she knew, Jacob still existed somewhere. She knew that those blips and pulses of energy that made up his body still existed somewhere in some form. They had existed since that one flickering instant when all creation rushed forth, a hurried breath, the first exhalation, the original unwinding. Those blips and pulses, spirals of sound and light, waves upon waves, points with no dimension, sighing about out amongst the clicks and whirrs and shimmers and howls, slowly cooling and sowing bits and pieces that would come together at various points as sand and light waves and Doric columns, rainwater in a culvert or white hair falling into a white sink, across all creation, through all history, of the Earth and elsewhere, to that small town to become her brother and they still existed out beyond the light of the parking lot, in one form or another, alive or dead, whole or disincorporated into nothing but dust and ash, but existing still, out in that very snow storm and she was part of that body and that blood and stood still beneath those harsh lights waiting for the man who claimed Jacob's name, who pulled Jacob's skin over his skin, to arrive and take all that she had. The first Word of all creation, carried across all time to a little boy in a tie standing outside alone, suddenly too far from home, the crumbling dust of stars, the silent reaches of space, the empty streets, the old homes covered in ivy, windows shattered, doors locked, the boy calling her name, calling, *Leah! Leah! Help me. Leeeeah!* She could hear him, his high voice outside as she sat inside the house, arms folded, angry and refusing to play along, Jacob yelling for his sister. All matter had conspired to stage that moment and Leah had refused it. How often had she listened to the night for that voice, to hear it one more time so that she could run to the window and call out to it, to run outside and see him and save him, this thing that she could never tell her parents, that she could never tell anyone. The vibrations of that voice, weakening and dissipating and eventually nothing more than the whisper of dry leaves on dead branches.

She was sobbing outside of the grocery store as the parking lot emptied. She stood in the bare light of the grocery store's sign, the leering head of a pig. Leah got into her blue VW and drove into the night and white wind eddied around her. But she could not wait forever. The snow was covering the road and the shoulders were already lost in the falling white. The snow flickered in the headlights as she sped down a country road and she thought about her parents' house, how it had looked when she was young with no furniture in the living room except for one wing-back chair, gold and purple, and how she and Jacob would play in that vast empty space, pretending it was their own private planet. The black night and the white sky and the lines of light writhing. The room mostly just held the shapes of the sun cut by the window panes as they moved across the floor, mutating from rhombus to rectangle to rhombus, which they would sit on when winded from wrestling. The black night and the white sky and the muffled growling of the tires. The sky was clear and poured in through the windows like water from a cracked aquarium, fizzy streams eager to escape from one world to the next. Bathed in light the children felt slower than anything. Their toys scattered and Jacob holding the toy car she'd given him for Christmas. The one he insisted on sleeping with. The black night and the white sky, the sky white from the gleaming falling the headlights breathing them aflame and the lights pulling up behind her. She would hide the car to make him cry and pretend she found it and he would throw his arms around his big sister and thank her. The cold on her neck turning for a moment and hearing him and seeing him disappear back into the dark night and the white sky writhing around her and the razor tongue of the evening wet islands of falling sky on her cheek and the radio still crooned old love careless love lost love gone honey gone dear gone forever they can be like we are. *Leah! Leeeah! Where is my car!*

Lost in the noise of the falling snow, Leah lost control of her car. It fishtailed as she overcorrected, terribly present in the moment, aware of what was happening and then the car left the road, she could feel that there was nothing around her for a moment, and then came to rest, nose down, in a ditch on the side of the road. She listened for a moment, felt a dull pain in her side where her seatbelt caught her and turned the car's engine off. It clicked as it cooled. She groaned. After several minutes, she regained her breath and then reached into her pocket for her cell phone. Her pocket was empty. She leaned forward and scanned the floor of the car, but didn't see it. She got out, tried to get on her hands and knees and search the floor of the car, but her side hurt too much. She was panting. Her lips were wet. She touched them and her fingers were daubed in blood.

A car was coming. She saw the rays of the headlights crowning the crest of the ditch. She walked up to the road and saw the car coming and waved for it to stop. It came to a halt a dozen yards from where she stood. It sat there idling for a moment and then the driver got out and walked around the front of the car. Leah called out to him, thanked him for stopping. He stood in the beams of the headlights and Leah could not discern his features beyond that he was balding and wearing thick-framed glasses. The headlights lit wild strands around his ears. She called to him again but he didn't respond. The man was singing to himself, softly, Leah was certain of it, or perhaps his stereo was still on in his car, and though Leah could hear what he was singing, felt a glimmer of recognition in the melody, she could not place it, but she thought of Jacob lying in his bed, counting the cars that passed the bedroom that they shared and she called out to him.

"Hello?" The man didn't move. The melody and his lights like the lights across the cracks of their ceiling. "I've had an accident." The melody and the light and something inside of her unwound and her hands were trembling. They remained like this for a moment, the man's shadow long between them, a faint song, Leah feeling more and more pain creeping through her body, the melody just out of reach, his shadow like a carpet laid out before her. He stood there and she could see his chest moving slightly with each breath in to wide cage of his chest and she felt faint for a moment and her body swam.

With a jolt she was aware that she'd become lost in some long thought, but abruptly felt sharp-edged and alert. She looked at the man. He'd taken a few steps, closing the gap between them. His hands were behind his back. He'd stopped singing. The music was gone. There was only the sound of his engine idling and nothing else. She could see nothing beyond the horizon of his headlights. All that existed were these few feet of gravel shoulder buried in new snow, the streaks of snow falling between them, tiny fires in the highbeams, and his shadow at the center of it. She took a step toward him, her pain gone, her body no longer trembling. As she moved toward him, he retreated, moving back to the side of his car. She called to him again, her voice rough and cracked. "What do you want?" A salt crowned crest rose in her and she repeated her question, a warm rush of blood in her throat. The blood and grime felt filthy on her hands. She could feel the drying smears on her face. She tried to wipe it off of her face with the back of her hand, but only succeeded in making her skin more aware of it. Something told her that her back hurt, that it wanted to bend, but she couldn't feel it. She stood straight and breathed the cold air's metal twang and started to laugh. It felt as though her mouth was wrenched wide open and that she was crawling out of herself. Her fingers curled into fists because they could think of no other shape.

With a fumbling rush, the man turned and got back into his car and slowly drove past her and on down the road. She flailed her arms, screaming at him, pounding on the side of the car as it passed, yet he continued. She leaned down and tried to look into his car at him, to see who it was, but the interior was dark and she could see nothing more than the dashboard lights reflected in his glasses for a brief moment. He wasn't even looking at her.

Twin gashes, twin pools of blood, twin dying lights as the car disappeared on the road and Leah, knowing these roads, knowing that the black line of country road would fade white and glittering in the distant night coming, she pulled her coat up tight, relieved to be alone. Twin lights dying and she walked along the edge of the road in the growing snow back toward the distant dome of Crow Station's artificial light reflected against the low sky. And she touched her neck. And she walked and she sang now too as the waves of snow flooded in around her, but she rose against them, faster and faster toward the unseen surface, toward an unknown light. And she touched her shoulder which roared and she rose against the sharp tongues of the wind and knives of the night. And she touched her lips and she said *O Jacob* as she walked along the road and walked along the road, the song now in her head and on her lips, smeared and screaming, though she did not know the song, now singing *O Jacob*, she made a new song, a new melody and new words, made them up as she walked and her body sang thunderbolts of pain with each step. And she remembered when the sky was clear and open and her father was coming down the stairs and her mother was calling her name and someone was knocking on the front door and she remembered the cars passing by the window of the room she shared with her brother where they counted the shifting shapes and she sang him to sleep. In the distance down the road, she could see lights approaching.

EPILOGUE: THE NEIGHBORHOOD CHILDREN

The boys, howling. Fireworks and strange words. The boys with long hair and rough breath. Leah watched them caper off and holding Jacob's hand, she walked him home, feeling his wet, small fingers, feeling the ruin of another lost Saturday, the sun already on the wane, feeling the slow cessation of his tears, and feeling for a moment a sudden writhing of pity and sorrow, and she bent down and held him, his wet clothes soaking her, the smell of dank water on both of them, and said she was sorry sorry sorry and somewhere they still heard the boys howling, their voices singing songs to burn down the coming night.

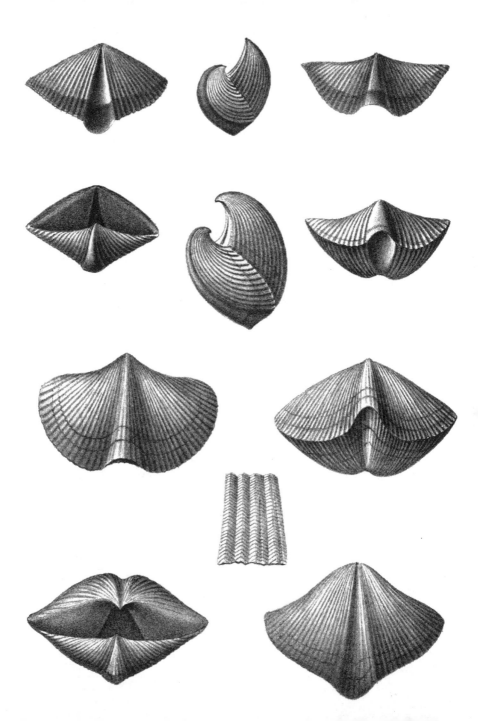

THANK YOU: Jennifer Connerley; Paige Stevens, Alex Stevens; Rick and Sandy Nahm; JD Dyche, RW Dyche; Todd Nahm, Laura Lewis, Mary Robert Garrett; Charles and Tamara Lockard, Megan Knagge; Robert Biggers, Finn Cohen, Jim Higdon, Matt Kalb, Clint Newman, John Norris, Eric Roehrig, Ben Spiker, Michael Turner; Kathryn Lofton; Helen Emmitt, Mark Lucas, Milton Reigelman; Eric Obenauf and Eliza Jane Wood-Obenauf; Patrick Mortensen, Steph Cha; the City of Danville, Kentucky.

Also published by **TWO DOLLAR RADIO**

CRYSTAL EATERS
A NOVEL BY SHANE JONES

"A powerful narrative that touches on the value of every human life, with a lyrical voice and layers of imagery and epiphany." —*BuzzFeed*

"[Jones is] something of a millennial Richard Brautigan." —*Nylon*

A QUESTIONABLE SHAPE
A NOVEL BY BENNETT SIMS

"[*A Questionable Shape*] is more than just a novel. It is literature. It is life." —*The Millions*

"Presents the yang to the yin of Whitehead's *Zone One*, with chess games, a dinner invitation, and even a romantic excursion." —*The Daily Beast*

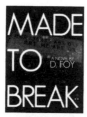

MADE TO BREAK
A NOVEL BY D. FOY

"With influences that range from Jack Kerouac to Tom Waits and a prose that possesses a fast, strange, perennially changing rhythm that's somewhat akin to some of John Coltrane's wildest compositions." —*HTML Giant*

RADIO IRIS
A NOVEL BY ANNE-MARIE KINNEY

"Kinney is a Southern California Camus." —*Los Angeles Magazine*

"[*Radio Iris*] has a dramatic otherworldly payoff that is unexpected and triumphant." —*New York Times Book Review*, Editors' Choice

THE ORANGE EATS CREEPS
A NOVEL BY GRACE KRILANOVICH

* National Book Foundation 2010 '5 Under 35' Selection.
* *NPR* Best Books of 2010.
* *The Believer* Book Award Finalist.

"Krilanovich's work will make you believe that new ways of storytelling are still emerging from the margins." —*NPR*

Also published by **TWO DOLLAR RADIO**

THE DROP EDGE OF YONDER
A NOVEL BY RUDOLPH WURLITZER

✳ *Time Out New York*'s Best Book of 2008.

✳ *ForeWord* Magazine 2008 Gold Medal in Literary Fiction.

"A picaresque American *Book of the Dead*... in the tradition of Thomas Pynchon, Joseph Heller, Kurt Vonnegut, and Terry Southern." —*Los Angeles Times*

HOW TO GET INTO THE TWIN PALMS
A NOVEL BY KAROLINA WACLAWIAK

"One of my favorite books this year." —*The Rumpus*

"Waclawiak's novel reinvents the immigration story."
—*New York Times Book Review*, Editors' Choice

THE CAVE MAN
A NOVEL BY XIAODA XIAO

✳ *WOSU* (NPR member station) Favorite Book of 2009.

"As a parable of modern China, [*The Cave Man*] is chilling."
—*Boston Globe*

THE PEOPLE WHO WATCHED HER PASS BY
A NOVEL BY SCOTT BRADFIELD

"Challenging [and] original... A billowy adventure of a book. In a book that supplies few answers, Bradfield's lavish eloquence is the presiding constant." —*New York Times Book Review*

"Brave and unforgettable. Scott Bradfield creates a country for the reader to wander through, holding Sal's hand, assuming goodness."
—*Los Angeles Times*

I'M TRYING TO REACH YOU
A NOVEL BY BARBARA BROWNING

✳ *The Believer* Book Award Finalist

"I think I love this book so much because it contains intimations of the potential of what books can be in the future, and also because it's hilarious." —Emily Gould, *BuzzFeed*

MIRA CORPORA
A NOVEL BY JEFF JACKSON

"This novel is like nothing I've ever read before and is, unquestionab one of my favorite books published this year." — *Salon*

"A piercing howl of a book. This punk coming-of-age story smolders long after the book is through." —*Slate*

SOME THINGS THAT MEANT THE WORLD TO ME
A NOVEL BY JOSHUA MOHR

* *O, The Oprah Magazine* '10 Terrific Reads of 2009.'

"Charles Bukowski fans will dig the grit in this seedy novel, a poetic rendering of postmodern San Francisco." —*O, The Oprah Magazine*

NOTHING
A NOVEL BY ANNE MARIE WIRTH CAUCHON

"Apocalyptic and psychologically attentive. I was moved." —Tao Lin, *New York Times Book Review*

"A riveting first piece of scripture from our newest prophet of misspent youth." —*Paste*

CRAPALACHIA
A NOVEL BY SCOTT MCCLANAHAN

"[McClanahan] aims to lasso the moon… He is not a writer of half-measures. The man has purpose. This is his symphony, every note designed to resonate, to linger." —*New York Times Book Review*

"*Crapalachia* is the genuine article: intelligent, atmospheric, raucously funny and utterly wrenching." —*The Washington Post*

SEVEN DAYS IN RIO
A NOVEL BY FRANCIS LEVY

"The funniest American novel since Sam Lipsyte's *The Ask*." —*Village Voice*

"Like an erotic version of Luis Bunuel's *The Discreet Charm of the Bourgeoisie*." —*The Cult*

O n an overcast Wednesday afternoon, Patrick N. Allen took his own life. He is survived by his father, Patrick, Sr.; his stepmother, Patricia; his step-sister, Patty; and his twin brother, Seth.

Coming 2015
Written & Directed by Eric Obenauf

P art-thriller, part-nightmarish examination of the widening gap between originality and technology, told with remarkable precision. Haunting and engaging, *The Removals* imagines where we go from here.

Coming 2015
Written by Nicholas Rombes
Directed by Grace Krilanovich